A King Production presents…

A Titillating Tale

A Novelette

Joy Deja King

This novelette is a work of fiction. Any references to real people, events, establishments, or locales are intended only to give the fiction a sense of reality and authenticity. Other names, characters, and incidents occurring in the work are either the product of the author's imagination or are used fictitiously, as those fictionalized events and incidents that involve real persons. Any character that happens to share the name of a person who is an acquaintance of the author, past or present, is purely coincidental and is in no way intended to be an actual account involving that person.

ISBN 13: 978-1-958834-90-9
ISBN 10: 1-958834-90-4
Cover concept by Joy Deja King
Library of Congress Cataloging-in-Publication Data;
A King Production
Mastermind 3...Callie's Cartel by Joy Deja King
Typesetting: www.anitaart79.wixsite.com/bookdesign

For complete Library of Congress Copyright info visit;
www.joydejaking.com
Twitter @joydejaking

A King Production
P.O. Box 912, Collierville, TN 38027
A King Production and the above portrayal log are trademarks of A King Production LLC

Copyright © 2025 by A King Production LLC. All rights reserved. No part of this book may be reproduced in any form without the permission from the publisher, except by reviewer who may quote brief passage to be printed in a newspaper or magazine.

This Novelette is Dedicated To My:

Family, Readers and Supporters.
I LOVE you guys so much. Please believe that!!

~ Joy Deja King ~

A special THANK YOU to my amazing sister Robin, for being the inspiration for this titillating tale.

~ Joy Deja King ~

"It Was All My Design
'Cause I'm A Mastermind ..."

Prologue...

Callie

The One Who Got Away

The scent of expensive perfume lingered in the air, but Callie Morgan felt anything but elegant. She sat at the edge of her king-sized bed, her fingers trembling as she held Cartier's engagement announcement in her lap. The hospital photo of him slipping that ring on Serenity's finger was burned into her mind like a brand.

Donovan leaned against the doorframe, arms crossed, eyes sharp with concern. "You gotta let this go, Callie. Cartier's moved on."

Callie looked up slowly. Her voice was low, dangerous. "Cartier doesn't belong to her. He never did. He's mine."

Donovan sighed, but didn't argue. He knew better. He'd seen that look in Callie's eyes before—right before she torched someone's life and walked away without blinking. Callie didn't lose. Not when it mattered.

"They think they won," she continued, her tone cold and calculating. "Lila's locked up, Serenity's playing queen, and Cartier's ready to rebuild his empire like nothing ever happened. But I'm not some chapter he can just close."

"So, what's your plan?" Donovan asked warily.

Callie's eyes gleamed. "I'm going to create something bigger than CR Enterprises. A company of my own. I've reached out to several members of the cartel. With the right power behind me, Cartier will come running back. And when he does..." Her lips curled into a slow, wicked smile. "I'll make sure Serenity watches me take everything."

She stood and crossed the room, heels clicking like a war drum. "There's one thing Serenity forgot—before Cartier met her, I was the queen. And I'm getting my throne back."

Lila

Buried Ties

The clank of the prison gate echoed behind Lila Richardson as she sat in the dim corner of the visitors' room. Her orange jumpsuit hugged her frame like shackles, but she wore it with the dignity of a queen in exile. The world might have turned against her, but Lila never relied on mercy. She relied on leverage.

She unfolded a creased letter, her eyes scanning the familiar handwriting. It came from one of the few people who still owed her—someone with deep roots in a network Callie was desperate to revive. A name from the past, a player from the same cartel Callie now sought to rally.

Lila smirked bitterly. The irony didn't escape her. Callie—the woman she once called a sister—now trying to build an empire in the same underworld Lila helped her escape. But friendship hadn't mattered in the end.

Callie made her choice. She chose Cartier. She fell in love with Lila's husband and turned her back on their bond. So, Lila had done what she always did—she eliminated the threat. Callie going down with Cartier had been deliberate, a warning wrapped in betrayal.

Still, the cartel didn't care about friendship or loyalty. They cared about power, and Lila still had secrets. Secrets that could buy her way out of prison—if played correctly.

Callie might have the streets behind her now, but Lila? Lila had the past in her pocket. And the past always comes calling.

Chapter One

The Leverage Game

The skyline of Atlanta glowed gold in the late evening light as Callie stood by the floor-to-ceiling windows of her new high-rise suite in Buckhead. The penthouse was sleek and minimal—fresh, clean, untouched. A blank canvas. Just like her future.

Callie had been released from jail for a few months, and she wasn't wasting time. She didn't do healing. She did rebuilding. And she'd already chosen a name for the empire she would rise from the ashes: Claymore Industries.

Behind her, Donovan placed two glasses of wine on the glass table and sat on the modern white leather couch. He watched her silently, a quiet war of loyalty unfolding in his eyes.

"So," Donovan finally said, "you're really doing this. Building your own company to compete with CR Enterprises."

Callie turned to face him; one brow raised. "Why do you sound surprised?"

He shrugged. "I'm not. I'm just wondering if it's about business… or Cartier."

She walked over, took the glass, and sat beside him. "It's about respect. Power. Control. And yeah… a little bit of Cartier." She smirked. "Don't act brand new."

Donovan leaned forward, resting his elbows on his knees. "Callie, I'll help you with the business. You know I got you. You're family to me. But I can't be a part of anything that directly targets Serenity."

Her smile faded slightly.

"You and Serenity got close while I was locked up," she said, voice flat.

He nodded. "We did. She risked everything to prove you, and Cartier was innocent. She was loyal—to both of you. Even when people doubted her. Even when I told her to stop."

Callie sighed and looked away; the tension thick between them.

"I'm not asking you to choose sides," she said after a pause. "You're my best friend. I just need help getting Claymore Industries off the ground. That's it."

Donovan looked her in the eyes. "Then promise me something. Promise me you won't drag me into whatever scheme you've got planned to break up Serenity and Cartier."

A beat passed.

"I promise," Callie said, her tone soft, eyes wide with innocence.

But as Donovan relaxed beside her and reached for his wine, Callie's mind was already racing.

She knew who she was.

And she knew what she wanted.

She just wouldn't let Donovan see it—until it was too late.

The walls of Fulton County Jail didn't scare Lila Richardson. What terrified others, she manipulated. What controlled others, she studied and rewired.

She wasn't waiting for justice. She was waiting for the right moment.

That moment came with a small knock—a coded tap on the metal bars of her cell.

A guard slipped her a sealed envelope, no words exchanged. He didn't meet her eyes. He didn't need to. Money still talked, even behind steel and concrete.

Lila opened the envelope with a flick of her manicured fingers. Inside was a burner phone and a torn page from an old bible, scrawled with a name she hadn't heard in over a decade: "Nikko."

She smirked.

Nikko ran with the old crew Callie was now trying to revive. Lila had once saved his sister from a deadly overdose when they were teenagers—he owed her. Big. And Lila never cashed in favors until it meant something.

She typed a short text into the burner:

I need a visit. Tell Nikko it's urgent. Remind him what I buried for him.

She leaned back on the bunk, crossing one leg over the other like she was still seated in Cartier's old boardroom. Let Callie think she was building something. Let Serenity enjoy her diamond ring. They were all playing the short game.

Lila was playing for keeps.

The Richardson estate was quiet—too quiet for Cartier's taste. Sunlight filtered in through the massive floor-to-ceiling windows, dancing across the polished marble floors. Serenity moved through the kitchen in silk lounge pants and a fitted tee, humming softly as she poured orange juice into two crystal glasses.

Cartier entered behind her, shirtless, his tattoos stark against his smooth brown skin. He kissed her cheek, watching the way she smiled without looking up.

"You seem happy," he said.

"I am," Serenity replied. "I just... keep waiting for the other shoe to drop."

Cartier leaned against the counter. "You've been through hell. You're allowed to be suspicious of peace."

She handed him his glass, her eyes searching his face. "Do you ever think about them?"

A pause.

"Lila and Callie?" he asked.

She nodded.

Cartier took a slow sip. "Of course I do. I share a lot of history with both. But they made choices... ones I couldn't forgive. And you—" He paused, setting the glass down. "You never gave up on me, even when I hated you for what I thought you did."

Serenity's throat tightened. "I didn't do it for forgiveness. I did it because it was right."

Cartier stepped closer, lifting her chin. "And now I'm right where I want to be."

They kissed—softly at first, then deeper. But just as Serenity melted into his arms, her phone buzzed.

She pulled away slowly and checked the screen. Her smile faded.

"What is it?" Cartier asked.

Serenity stared at the text:

Callie Morgan just registered Claymore Industries LLC. Filed: Atlanta, GA.

Chapter Two

Snakes In The Shadows

Nikko entered the Fulton County Jail visitor's room wearing a dark hoodie, his face partially hidden, but his eyes—sharp, calculating—never missed a detail. He sat across from Lila, who looked effortlessly composed despite the jumpsuit and the fluorescent lights above her.

"Took you long enough," Lila cracked.

"You said it was urgent," Nikko replied. "So, talk."

"I want out," Lila said flatly. "Before trial."

Nikko snorted. "You think I can wave a wand and make your charges disappear?"

"I think you can reach the right people. I think you've still got pull. And I know things… about Callie. About the people she's trying to recruit."

Nikko leaned forward, interested now. "Go on."

"You help me, I'll give you everything you need to control what she's building. If she gets in, you get boxed out. But if we move together…" Her eyes narrowed. "You get the power. I get my freedom."

"And what makes you think I won't just use your info and leave you here?"

Lila smiled coldly. "Because I still have the recording from when your crew raided that tech startup in Midtown. I protected you then. I can destroy you now."

Nikko sat back, quiet for a long moment. "I'll make a call."

As he stood to leave, Lila's voice followed him.

"Oh—and tell Callie," eyes glittering, "the past is coming for her."

Mastermind 3...

The conference room at Callie's temporary headquarters was buzzing with activity—young professionals, fresh out the game or corporate sharks looking for a new empire to align with. She was building Claymore Industries brick by brick, and every detail mattered.

Donovan stood by the whiteboard reviewing logistics when Callie's burner phone lit up. Only a few people had that number.

She answered quickly. "Yeah?"

A voice on the other end, raspy and low. "You need to know something. Lila's moving behind bars. She made contact with Nikko."

Callie's blood ran cold.

"Nikko?" she repeated. "Why the hell would she reach out to him?"

"She's offering leverage. Trying to buy her way out of prison with your name in her mouth. Saying she's got dirt on you... maybe more."

The line clicked dead.

Callie stared at the phone, her jaw tightening.

Donovan looked up. "Something wrong?"

She hesitated—then forced a calm expression. "Nothing I can't handle."

But inside, her mind was racing. Lila. That name still made her stomach turn. After all these years, after the betrayal, after prison... Lila still wanted control. Still wanted to pull the strings. First Cartier. Now this?

Hell no.

Callie stood up abruptly. "Clear the room."

Donovan blinked. "Callie, we're in the middle of—

"I said clear it!" Her voice sliced through the room like a blade.

One by one, everyone filed out. When the door shut behind them, Callie turned to Donovan.

"She's reaching out to people from the past. Trying to sabotage me before I even get started."

"Who?"

"Lila."

Donovan's face darkened. "From inside prison?"

"She's desperate," Callie said, pacing. "But smart. If she gets Nikko on her side, she could disrupt everything I'm trying to build."

"So, what's the play?"

Callie turned; eyes blazing. "We remind Nikko who the hell I am. And we send Lila a message—loud and clear. This time, she's not the only one who knows how to bury people."

Fulton County Jail
10:43 a.m. – Pod C, Maximum Security Unit

Lila was finishing her black coffee—lukewarm, bitter—when a guard slipped a small envelope under her tray without a word.

She waited until he walked away. Inside was a single photo. A snapshot of Nikko. Leaning into Callie's ear at a downtown lounge. Callie's hand rested lightly on his thigh. Both of them smiling.

On the back of the photo, in Callie's unmistakable handwriting, were four words:

Nice try, bitch. Sit tight.

Lila's fingers curled around the photo so tightly it crinkled. Her jaw clenched. Her pulse pounded in her ears.

Callie wasn't bluffing—she was hitting back.

Lila inhaled slowly, forcing calm. Rage was a tool. Panic was a weakness. And Callie had just revealed her own hand.

"She still wants power," Lila muttered. "Still needs validation. Still playing emotional."

But Lila wasn't done. Not yet.

She stood and walked to the bulletin board outside her cell block—where messages were pinned from inmates to their visitors.

She tacked up her own note. Just one word on a torn envelope:

"Reignite."

The right people would know what it meant. Old debts. Old fires. If Callie wanted war, she'd get it. But not on her terms.

Chapter Three

The Warning and The Win

Nikko leaned against the sleek marble bar, sipping from a glass of D'USSÉ, when Callie approached in a curve-hugging blazer dress, heels clicking like a metronome of control.

"Enjoying yourself?" she asked smoothly.

He smiled, glancing around Claymore Industries 9th floor lounge in Midtown, Atlanta. "This place is impressive. Clean. Sharp. A little… too polished."

Callie poured herself a drink. "A queen can be lethal and refined."

"You're coming hard," Nikko said, watching her. "You trying to buy me or scare me?"

"Neither," Callie said, eyes cold. "I'm reminding you who built the pipeline you're standing on. You owe Lila, yeah—but you followed me."

Nikko raised a brow. "That was a long time ago."

She stepped in closer. "Then let me make it current."

From her clutch, she pulled a flash drive and placed it on the bar. "That's a full ledger. Crypto routing. Shipment access points. Untapped supplier contracts from Colombia and Ghana. You want leverage? I'm giving you your future."

He picked it up slowly. "And what do you want in return?"

She leaned in, her breath warm against his cheek. "Loyalty. Exclusivity. And silence."

Nikko chuckled. "You always did play the game with blood on your lipstick."

Callie smiled, her voice velvet and venom.

"And you always liked the taste."

Mastermind 3...

The soft sound of R&B played from the speakers in Serenity's office, but her mind wasn't on the music. She sat behind her sleek mahogany desk, reviewing acquisition projections, though the numbers blurred before her eyes.

She was still thinking about Callie.

The press had barely caught wind of Claymore Industries, but Serenity had already spotted the strategy: bold branding, aggressive recruitment, and whispers of a distribution channel that looked too calculated to be coincidental.

A knock at her door broke the silence.

"Come in," she called.

Donovan stepped inside. He wore tailored slacks and a crisp open-collar shirt, but his face carried tension.

"We need to talk," he said without preamble.

Serenity sat up straighter. "About what?"

"Callie."

Serenity hesitated, then gestured to the chair across from her. "Go ahead."

Donovan didn't sit. "She's not just trying to

build a company. She's trying to get Cartier back."

Serenity blinked. "Talk about getting straight to the point."

"I know you don't want to believe it," Donovan continued, "but she's obsessed. She thinks you stole the life she was supposed to have. That ring on your finger? It's a trigger. And she's not the type to sit back and let things play out."

Serenity's voice was calm, but her eyes hardened. "So, what are you saying? That she's coming for me?"

"I'm saying don't let your guard down. Callie will use charm, pity, business, sex—whatever she needs. And if Cartier so much as glances her way, she'll take that as a signal to strike."

Serenity exhaled slowly. "And where do you stand in all this?"

"I told her I'd help build her business—but I won't be part of her war with you. I'm here to put you on notice because you deserve to know what's coming."

Serenity nodded; her voice quiet. "I know how close you are to Callie, so thank you for being honest and the warning."

Donovan paused before turning to leave. "Just be careful, Serenity. She's playing the long game. And Callie doesn't lose."

"And neither do I," Serenity whispered to herself.

Fulton County Jail – Secured Block

Lila stood in the prison chapel; eyes locked on the stained-glass window as if searching for a divine sign. But faith had nothing to do with her next move—only strategy.

Behind her, two women entered the chapel—both inmates, loyal to her from another life. One had a serpent tattoo curling up her neck. The other had a razor scar under her left eye.

"They got the message," Razor said. "You were right. Nikko bent. He's with Callie now."

Lila didn't flinch. "Good. Let her think she won."

Tattoo raised a brow. "You don't sound mad."

"I'm not," Lila said smoothly. "I'm focused." She pulled a folded page from her pocket. "It's time for Plan B."

The women took it, scanning the scribbled names and coded phrases.

"You sure about this?" Razor asked. "I ain't corporate. I'ma killer."

"That's exactly why I need you," Lila replied. "Callie's playing business. I'm about to remind everyone where the real fear lives." She stepped back toward the altar, eyes sharp. "This city forgot what I'm capable of. Let's jog their memory."

Chapter Four

Loyalty Lines and Loaded Moves

Serenity stood by the bookshelf in the private study at Cartier's estate. Her arms folded and her eyes tracing the spines of his favorite first editions. But her thoughts were somewhere else.

"Donovan came to see you," Cartier said as he entered, interrupting her thoughts.

She turned, her expression unreadable. "He said Callie's trying to get you back."

He crossed the room, standing in front of her. "And what do you think?"

"I think I need to hear it from you," she whispered.

Cartier took her hand and guided her to the leather couch. The room was dim, the Atlanta city lights casting soft patterns across the floor.

"My relationship with Callie was complicated for many reasons," he said. "But I was also a very complicated man back then," Cartier admitted.

"Is that a diplomatic way of saying you were a womanizer?" Serenity asked.

"Let's just say, in the past I should have been more mindful of how I treated the women I was in a relationship with. That includes Lila and Callie. But to answer your question. If Callie wants me back, it's only because she's fixated on what she imagines it could have been, not the reality of what it truly was."

"I see."

"But with you, Serenity... you held me down when it mattered. When everyone turned their backs."

He reached out and brushed a strand of hair from her face.

"When I look at you, I see my future. Not my past. I strive to be a better man because you deserve the best of me."

She blinked slowly, emotion softening her expression. Cartier leaned in, lips brushing hers. Their kiss deepened—slow at first, then hungry, urgent. He lifted her effortlessly into his lap, her legs straddling him as she unbuttoned his shirt. Fingers tangled; breaths hitched. The tension melted into passion, their bodies moving in sync, both trying to silence the noise of the world outside these walls.

When it was over, they lay entangled, hearts pounding.

"You believe me now?" he asked, voice low.

Serenity nodded against his chest. "Yeah. I do."

But neither of them knew that war had already begun.

In the late hours at an auto shop in the Southside of Atlanta, the air smelled of rust, oil, and the kind of secrets that never stayed buried. A black Tahoe pulled in behind the closed gates, headlights flashing twice.

Inside the driver's seat, a mid-tier investor for Claymore Industries checked his watch. He was new to the game, thinking his money bought protection.

He didn't know his name had been passed down the chain… all the way back to Lila.

In a shadowed alley across the street, Razor stepped out, freshly released from Fulton County on "clerical grounds." Paperwork fumbled. Bail posted anonymously. Judge reassigned.

Lila's connections still had reach.

Razor moved like vapor, slipping through the gate before it even fully closed. The man never saw her coming.

One slash behind the knees. One whisper in his ear.

"Callie thinks she's untouchable. Lila disagrees."

He reached for his phone—but Razor buried the blade deep into his side before he could press send.

As he bled out beside his car, Razor carved a message into the hood with the tip of her blade:

The Queen is not done

She disappeared into the dark, leaving only blood, steel, and silence behind.

Mastermind 3...

Callie's assistant burst into the glass-walled conference room at Claymore Industries HQ pale and shaking. "You need to come downstairs," she stammered. "Now."

Callie looked up from her tablet. "What is it?"

"It's Malik. One of the investors... he's dead."

Callie stood slowly, every nerve in her body snapping to attention. "What do you mean dead?"

"They found him in his car outside of the auto shop across the street. Slashed open. And someone carved something into the hood."

Her voice dropped to a whisper. "It said: The Queen is not done."

The room fell silent.

Donovan, seated at the far end of the table, stood up. "Tell me that's not who I think it is."

Callie didn't answer. She was already walking—fast, heels clicking like gunfire on the sleek floors.

She reached the elevator, jabbing the button as rage churned in her chest.

Lila.

She'd underestimated her. She thought Lila would be scrambling, weak, forgotten behind bars. But this? This was a direct hit. A street-level chess move meant to destabilize, to terrorize. And it worked.

Once back upstairs, Donovan caught up with Callie before she entered her office.

"You need to slow down," he said. "This is the kind of thing that draws heat. If the police tie this back to your company—"

"They won't," Callie snapped. "Because I'm going to handle it before it gets that far."

Donovan's jaw clenched. "And what does that mean?"

"It means I'm going to send my own message to everyone, including Lila, that I didn't survive prison to play nice."

She stormed into her office, slamming the door. For the first time since Claymore Industries was born, Callie felt something she hadn't felt in a long time: Threatened. And she hated it.

Fulton County Jail

Lila sat on her bunk, one leg crossed elegantly over the other as she listened to the buzz of cell doors clanking and guards barking orders.

She didn't flinch when a note was slipped under her cell.

She opened it, smiling at the scrawl inside:

"Malik bled out like a bitch. Hood message delivered. ATL talking. – Razor."

Lila folded the note delicately, tucked it into her Bible, and whispered:

"Check."

Chapter Five

Retribution

It was dim, lit only by the glow of six oversized monitors feeding live security footage, street reports and encrypted messages, in what Callie called her private war room at Claymore Industries HQ. She sat at the head of the table, flanked by two of her most trusted lieutenants—Briggs and Nova.

"That was a bold message," Briggs said. "Old-school. Direct. You've made moves on the surface, but Lila? She's back in the shadows."

Callie exhaled slowly, her knuckles whitening around a gold pen. "Not anymore."

She tapped her fingers against a digital map of Atlanta. It lit up with red pins—each one connected to a Lila-aligned player from the old cartel days. Dealers, runners, shell business owners, street informants.

"I want every one of these people shut down. No product, no movement, no noise. Cut off the oxygen."

Nova leaned in. "You think that'll stop Razor?"

"I'm not stopping Razor," Callie said coldly. "I'm isolating her."

Her eyes locked on a blinking red dot at the edge of the map. Southside Safehouse #3.

"Lila's pulling strings, but she's still in prison. She's using Razor and whoever's still loyal. That's her mistake—trusting old blood."

Briggs smirked. "So, what's the play?"

"We bleed them dry," Callie said. "Quietly. No bodies, no noise. Just power. I want every street whisper to say the same thing: Claymore controls the game now."

Fulton County Jail – Infirmary Wing, 2nd Floor

Lila adjusted the blanket on her lap, feigning illness. The prison infirmary was the one place with spotty guard rotation and soft surveillance. She wasn't sick—she was strategic.

Across from her sat a heavyset woman in a janitor's uniform, eyes sharp beneath her dull expression.

"Your girl made a move," the woman said. "Three of your old connects were pulled from the pipeline. One is in hiding. Two other flipped. Word is, Callie's locking down your whole base."

Lila didn't flinch. "Good. That means she's scared."

The janitor hesitated. "You want me to hit something back?"

"No," Lila replied. "We don't fight that kind of fire with fire. Callie's using business. So now I will too."

She reached into her blanket and slid a flash drive wrapped in plastic across the table.

The janitor eyed the item warily.

Lila smirked. "Relax. It came in last week—tucked inside a hollowed-out Bible sent from one of my old contacts in D.C. Chaplain never looked twice. Who'd expect the word of God to carry the keys to a takedown?"

The janitor shook her head, impressed despite herself. "And you just happened to have dirt on Callie tucked away for all these years?"

"I'm a Richardson," Lila said, calm and cold. "I've always kept receipts. She just never thought I'd cash them in while locked behind bars."

She slid the drive forward with purpose. "Leak it. Channel 2. Let them light the match. That's all the dirt on Claymore Industries' shell investors—every skeleton Callie tried to bury before going legit. Anonymous tip. Straight to the press."

The janitor's eyes widened. "You sure? That's nuclear."

"Exactly. Let's see how clean her empire looks once the world sees the bones it was built on."

The janitor hesitated over the flash drive, curiosity setting in. "Where did you get this, the information I mean?"

"Oh, you want to know where it came from?" Lila gave a wicked laugh, her voice full of amusement. "Back when Callie and I were still tight, I linked her up with someone who was an expert at cleaning up financial messes. Of course I made them keep copies—tax filings, off-the-book payments, even the fake identity of her original silent partner in Harlem. It was all tucked away, just in case. And I have more ammunition to unleash when the time it right," she winked.

The janitor's brow arched. "You were planning this from the beginning?"

"No," Lila said, leaning in. "But I never leave myself defenseless. Even when I pretend to."

She sat back, calm as a queen on a throne. "Now deliver it. Drop it to the biggest media outlet in Atlanta. Callie wants to act like she's a mogul. Let's see how she handles a scandal."

WSB-TV Channel 2 News – Breaking Report Atlanta, GA

"Good evening. We begin with a developing story involving the newly formed Claymore Industries, the brainchild of ex-con and former CR Enterprises executive Callie Morgan.

In a shocking twist, documents leaked late this afternoon reveal hidden investors with links to narcotics trafficking, money laundering, and falsified business filings. Sources claim these documents were sent anonymously to several media outlets. While authenticity is still being verified, the sheer volume of evidence is already sparking major investigations—both federal and local."

In the executive conference room at CR Enterprises, Cartier slammed the remote down on the table as the news anchor's voice faded.

Across from him, Serenity stared at the screen, stunned.

"She just launched two months ago," Serenity murmured. "How did this much dirt already surface?"

Cartier's jaw was tight. "Because it was planted. This isn't a media leak. It's a hit."

Serenity turned to him. "From who?"

He didn't even hesitate. "Lila."

"She's in jail."

"That's never stopped her before."

Serenity's mind raced. "If Claymore collapses, it won't just affect Callie. We share vendors. The CR brand is on boards and partnerships with companies linked to her. If this spirals…"

"We take a hit too," Cartier finished grimly.

A knock came at the door.

Spencer, Cartier's Chief of Staff walked in slowly, holding a tablet.

"Just got off the phone with Donovan. Callie knows," he said. "She saw the reports. And she's now planning damage control…"

Serenity stood. "What's she planning?"

Spencer looked at them both.

"Retaliation."

Chapter Six

Cut the Head, Starve the Snake

Callie stood with her arms crossed and an inscrutable expression, facing the massive flat-screen mounted to her office wall.. The screen showed a paused news clip of her name splashed across every outlet in bold letters:

"EX-CON EXEC LINKED TO UNDERWORLD FUNDING."

Behind her, Nova and Briggs remained silent. No one dared speak until Callie did.

"Where's the leak?" she finally asked, voice like ice.

Nova stepped forward with a tablet. "The metadata on the flash drive pointed back to a burner email routed through a proxy server. But whoever sent it had access to original documents from years ago—stuff no one had except your inner circle."

Callie's eyes narrowed. "So, it's not just some anonymous hacker?"

"No," Briggs said grimly. "This was personal."

Callie walked to her desk and pressed a hidden panel beneath the drawer. A concealed compartment clicked open, revealing a sleek black ledger notebook—old-school. Inside were handwritten names, contacts, dates. People who had been with her from the beginning.

She flipped through the pages until she stopped on one name.

"Delores Griggs." Her old financial cleaner from back when she was still ghosting money through shell salons in Harlem. "She went underground after my arrest. Said she was done," Callie murmured.

Nova frowned. "You think she flipped?"

Callie nodded slowly. "No—I think she sold

me out. Probably owes Lila something from back in the day. Or maybe she just saw a chance to cash in and disappear."

Briggs cracked his knuckles. "Want us to find her?"

"No," Callie said. "I'll do it myself."

Later that night, outside a dimly lit laundromat on Cascade Road, Delores didn't see her coming. She was halfway to her car, groceries in hand, when Callie stepped from the shadows in a sleek black trench coat and pointed heels sharp enough to stab through concrete.

"Hey Dee," Callie said softly. "Remember me?"

Delores froze. "Callie... I didn't know—"

Callie snatched the grocery bag from her arms and tossed it aside. "You think I wouldn't find out? You leaked my files. My business. To Lila of all people."

"I didn't have a choice," Delores whispered. "She threatened to expose my son—his past, his location. I had to protect him."

"You protected him," Callie echoed. "But you put a target on me."

Delores trembled. "I never thought she'd actually leak it—"

"She did. And now my name's in flames."

Callie stepped closer until they were nose to nose. "You're lucky I'm not the same woman I was in prison. But if you ever breathe my name again, I swear, I'll bury you."

She turned to walk away—then paused. "Oh, and Dee?"

Delores looked up.

"If my empire goes down, yours burns with it."

Fulton County Jail – Library Wing, 3:17 p.m.

The whisper came during Lila's afternoon reading hour, delivered by a trustee pretending to shelve books behind her.

"She found Delores."

Lila didn't even look up from the novel in her lap. "And?"

"Scared the woman half to death. Threatened to burn her whole life down."

Lila turned the page calmly. "She's still reactive. Still emotional. That's why she'll never win."

The trustee lingered. "Should I pull Dee out of the city?"

"No," Lila scoffed. "She served her purpose. Callie thinks she scared the truth out of her, but Delores was just a pawn."

She slid a marked page from the book—another coded message, this one scribbled in a cipher only Razor would understand.

"Take this to her," Lila said. "It's time to stop playing games in the dark."

The trustee hesitated. "You sure you wanna escalate? Razor's already hot."

Lila finally looked up, her stare sharp enough to draw blood.

"She's not there to survive, she's there to remind. Razor doesn't just kill. She sends a message."

She leaned forward, voice low and lethal.

"If Callie wants war, I'll give her Razor in the daylight."

Razor finished wrapping her fists in gauze, sweat slick on her chest as she hammered the heavy bag with a relentless rhythm. It was after midnight. The gym was empty except for shadows—exactly how she liked it.

Until she heard the door creak.

She paused, one hand still raised. "You must be crazy walking in here uninvited."

Callie's voice sliced through the air like a dagger. "You've been bleeding my business long enough. I figured it was time we met face to face."

Callie stepped forward under the flickering light, flanked by Nova and Briggs. Their silence was more threatening than words.

Razor grunted. "What? You here to talk me to death?"

Callie nodded once. That was all it took.

Briggs moved first, fast and clean—grabbing Razor from behind and locking her arms back. Nova stepped in, jamming a taser to Razor's side and triggering a brutal jolt that brought the enforcer to her knees.

Razor hissed in pain but refused to scream.

That's why Lila had always trusted her—she didn't break easy.

Callie approached slowly, crouching in front of her.

"You're not untouchable," she whispered, pulling a thin blade from her coat. "You were just the loudest distraction in a losing game."

She slid the tip of the blade across Razor's collarbone, shallow enough to avoid real damage—but deep enough to sting. Deep enough to scar.

Then she reached into her pocket, pulled out a blood-red napkin embossed with the CR Enterprises monogram, and placed it gently on Razor's chest.

"Tell your queen," Callie said coldly, "I replied to her message. Now here's mine—next time, I don't send a warning."

As she turned to walk away, Razor spat blood to the side and glared through the pain.

"You should've killed me."

Callie didn't even turn around. "No. I want you alive to remind her what losing feels like."

Chapter Seven

The Calm And The Kill

Fulton County Jail – Restricted Visitation Room

Lila sat motionless at the steel table; her manicured hands folded like a woman waiting for tea—not vengeance.

Across from her, a new enforcer stood silent. Younger. Clean-cut. Eyes colder than Razor's ever were.

The prison guard outside the door had been paid to turn the cameras off for ten minutes.

"Razor failed," the enforcer said. "Word is Callie marked her. Left her alive as a warning."

Lila smiled, slow and dangerous. "Good. Now she knows this isn't about bullets. It's about legacy."

She slid a sealed envelope across the table.

"Deliver this to Councilman Bryce," she said. "He owes me. I want zoning blocks paused on every Claymore-linked property within city limits. No permits. No approvals. Not a brick laid."

The enforcer took the envelope without a word.

Lila's eyes glittered. "Claymore Industries will represent another major failure for Callie. I will make sure she never has an opportunity to celebrate. Callie will be picking up the pieces after it crumbles."

Serenity stood by the boardroom window, watching reporters gather outside the CR Enterprises building. Their presence had increased every day since the Claymore leak. Questions were circling: Were CR and Claymore connected? Had Cartier known about the illegal investors?

Cartier entered, tossing a thick file on the table. "Our PR firm just bailed."

"Another one?" Serenity asked, exhausted.

"They said we're too tainted right now. Not enough distance between us and Callie."

She turned. "You think we're going to lose board members?"

Cartier didn't answer right away. ""We've weathered worse. However, our company is only starting to bounce back from my incarceration and the criminal trial. If another scandal hits… it could be the start of something bigger."

Serenity's voice was low. "And she's not finished."

"No," Cartier said. "She's just getting comfortable."

Callie poured herself a glass of champagne and stepped out onto the rooftop terrace at Claymore Industries Midtown Headquarters. The Atlanta skyline glittered beneath her feet like it belonged to her.

Briggs joined her, nodding. "Construction teams are back in place. That citywide zoning freeze Lila tried to pull. Dead in the water."

"Excellent," Callie said. "Every time she moves, we cut deeper."

Nova appeared with a tablet. "Razor's been silent. No retaliation. No moves from Lila since your visit."

Callie beamed. "Let's reward ourselves," she said. "How about we plan a celebration."

Nova grinned. "What kind?"

"The kind people remember. Press. Celebs. Influencers. High fashion. I want this city dripping in gold, champagne, and envy."

She turned to look at the city again, eyes glowing with power.

"I want everyone in Atlanta to know: Claymore isn't rising. Claymore has arrived."

Callie's team promptly began preparing for what she expected to be the party of the year. Ever the architect of spectacle, she orchestrated her operation with a precision most military tacticians would envy. There were men in tailored black bustling with crates of imported champagne, florists weaving hothouse orchids into improbable shapes, sound technicians dangling spider-like from the mezzanine while scrutinizing the acoustics. Silk linens were steamed and draped; rare caviars and custom sushi were plated with mathematical exactitude. Callie would not stand for even the slightest deviation from perfection.

She insisted, with her signature blend of charm and threat, on examining every detail—the temperature of the canapés, the cut of the ice cubes, the scent of the candles (oud, not vanilla, never vanilla). No assistant dared falter. This was not just a party: it was a declaration. The city would remember this night, and Callie would slip further into the mythology of Atlanta's social scene, all diamond-hard poise and auburn hair. If all went as planned, with Cartier by her side.

A week before the party, Callie twirled in a floor-length designer gown, deep emerald with a thigh-high slit. "Too much?" she asked, her grin gleaming.

Nova snapped a photo. "It's perfection. And exactly what you need."

Fashion magazines had already requested exclusives. Bloggers buzzed about the event, calling it "Atlanta's most elite relaunch." Callie wasn't just building a company—she was branding her resurrection. Champagne towers, a runway of power, and an invite-only guest list.

Even Donovan, though still loyal, raised an eyebrow at the opulence. "You really want to flex this hard?"

Callie smirked. "After what I survived? I don't flex. I arrive."

Behind the scenes, Briggs ran background checks on every vendor, performer, and guest. He had the team on lockdown. Callie thought of everything...

Except Lila.

Lila sat quietly as the mail cartwheeled past her. A folded flyer caught her eye: Claymore: The Official Black & Gold Empire Launch. Location: The Eden Vault – Buckhead. Guest List: Closed.

She didn't speak. Didn't flinch. Just took it.

Later that evening, alone in her cell, she reached into the hollowed-out spine of the novel beside her bunk and pulled out a napkin. Hidden inside was a small USB drive—one of the two pieces Delores had smuggled in weeks ago, when she'd delivered the original flash drive with Claymore's investor records.

Lila had waited to use this one. The nuclear option.

Tucked beside it was a single note, in Razor's handwriting:

"Servers. Midnight. Stream it live. They'll never forget."

Lila traced the edge of the USB, then folded the napkin back up with care.

"Let her glitter," she murmured. "I'll give them something else to watch."

Spotlights danced across The Eden Vault. A private rooftop oasis had been transformed into a dream—black roses, gold accents, champagne flowing, camera flashes popping. Music pulsed. A-list influencers clinked glasses with local royalty.

Callie stood at the top of the grand staircase, dressed in gold, a custom crown of gilded thorns resting on her head. The crowd erupted as she descended.

"Claymore is the future," she declared. "Tonight, we don't just celebrate—we claim what's ours."

Applause thundered.

But twelve floors below, in the private server room—accessible only by a contractor badge someone had sold for $10,000 in Bitcoin—an unmarked device blinked to life. It uploaded.

Encrypted files were released to a network of IPs. Financial records. Name swaps. Whistleblower footage. But most damning? A silent video.

Callie, months earlier, inside a prison visitation booth… whispering to a man on the inside.

A known trafficker.

The same name linked to one of Claymore's shell companies.

Back upstairs, seconds later…one by one, phones buzzed. Screens lit up. Guests began turning. Murmuring.

Nova checked hers and froze.

"Callie," she said. "You need to see this—"

Then, the music cut out. And on the massive LED display behind the stage, the video played. Callie. Behind glass. Whispering. Smiling. The footage was clean. Undeniable. And the party? Over.

Chapter Eight

Desperation Tastes Like Dust

The morning after the party, the once-buzzing lobby of Claymore Industries was dead silent. The front desk had been vacated. Reporters and protestors swarmed outside like vultures.

Inside, Callie stood barefoot in her office, still wearing last night's gold gown—now wrinkled, mascara streaking her face like war paint.

"If I had realized the media would be gathered outside the office building, I would have chosen to stay in a hotel suite rather than taking shelter in my office," Callie grumbled.

Nova paced in front of the blacked-out windows, phone in hand. "Investors are pulling out. Social media is scorched. Hashtags like #ClaymoreCorrupt and #CartelCallie are trending in every major market."

"Damage control?" Callie asked hoarsely.

Briggs shook his head. "No PR firm will touch you. You're toxic. This wasn't a smear campaign—this was an execution."

Callie gripped the edge of her glass desk, knuckles pale.

"I should've killed Lila when I had the chance," she whispered.

Nova looked at her. "What do you want to do?"

Callie straightened slowly, pain giving way to cold calculation. "I want to end this."

She turned toward the closet in her office, changed into a sleek black suit, pulled her hair into a tight ponytail, and slipped on her Louboutin stilettos like armor.

Briggs frowned. "Where are you going? Don't you think you should fix your face?"

"To the one person Lila can't touch," she

said. "And the only man who might be able to save what I have left." Callie paused at the door, "Oh, and my face can wait," she snapped before storming out.

The estate, located on the outskirts of Atlanta, belonging to the leader of a prominent cartel, resembled a fortress with its gates and surveillance cameras. Guards flanked the marble entrance, resembling soldiers ready for war.

Callie's Maybach was searched. Her phone confiscated. She was escorted into a sunken courtyard draped in shadow and silence.

At the head of a long onyx table sat Emilio Vega—a ghost in most circles, a divinity in others. The top of the cartel. The one Lila once feared. The one who'd disappeared when the game got too messy. Until now.

He didn't rise when she entered. Didn't offer a seat.

"I thought you were trying to go legit," Emilio remarked, his voice steady yet edged with resolve.

"I was," Callie said. "But you know better than anyone... sometimes the streets follow you."

He studied her. "So why are you here?"

Callie took a breath, burying her pride.

"Because I need your help. Someone leaked footage from before Claymore even launched—painted me as still in the life. Now they're trying to kill everything I built."

Emilio sipped from a glass of dark rum. "You built your house on cartel sand, Callie. And now you want the tide to stop rising?"

"I need protection," she said. "Resources. Political leverage. Enough to shift public attention before the feds move in."

He stared at her for a long time, then finally said:

"Lila?"

"Yes."

Emilio leaned back, steepling his fingers.

"Then you better be ready to pay. In loyalty. In silence. And in blood."

Callie remained stoic. "I already gave up everything else."

The air in the room quickly turned thick with cigar smoke and consequence. Callie sat across from Emilio Vega now, the silence between them taut as a wire ready to snap.

She hadn't touched the drink offered. She knew better. This was a test—and it was only just beginning.

"You want my protection," Emilio said at last, "but protection in my world isn't a shield—it's a contract."

"I understand," Callie replied, her voice steady.

"You say that," Emilio said, "but you left this life once. Went clean. Built a brand, got press. You forgot what loyalty costs."

"I never forgot." Callie stated. "I just hoped I'd never have to come back."

Emilio tapped ash from his cigar. "Then let's make things plain."

He stood and walked to a vault built into the wall, entering a code only he knew. When it opened, he pulled out a thin black folder and dropped it in front of her.

Callie opened it slowly.

Inside were photos. Names. Addresses. A list of city officials, media gatekeepers, and corporate insiders—all tied to her takedown.

"Some of them were flipped by Lila," Emilio said. "Some were already dirty. All of them need to disappear."

Callie felt a lump in her throat. "Disappear?"

Emilio smiled without warmth. "Your empire crumbled before it was even fully constructed because people don't fear you. I'll fix that. But I need you to make one of these names disappear. Personally."

Callie's heart thudded in her chest.

"You're serious."

"I don't bluff," he said. "Pick one. Make a statement. Or walk out of here with nothing. And next time Lila strikes, you'll be alone."

She stared at the photos. Her hand trembled as she hovered over one name in particular.

Zaire Monroe — the media exec who greenlit the broadcast of her prison footage.

She remembered his smug interview. His smile. The betrayal.

Callie looked back up at Emilio. She hadn't been opposed to the idea of murder, but the thought of actually committing the act herself filled her with dread. Callie wasn't inclined to have Zaire's blood on her hands.

"If I do this," she said, "I'm in. No backing out."

Emilio's eyes glinted with finality. "Exactly. That's the price."

Chapter Nine

The Edge of Extinction

Fulton County Jail – Private Attorney Visitation Room

Lila sat across from her lawyer, but this wasn't a legal meeting. Her real business was in the manila envelope just placed on the table.

She opened it and smiled.

Inside were high-resolution photos of Callie walking into Emilio Vega's estate.

"You were right," the lawyer said. "She went back to him."

"She always does," Lila murmured. "Desperation makes people predictable."

She scanned the rest of the contents—surveillance of Callie's team tracking Zaire Monroe, reports of cartel operatives moving in Atlanta's media circle, even chatter from her own plants inside City Hall.

"She's been tasked with eliminating Zaire," the lawyer added. "And she's stalling."

Lila closed the folder and leaned back, triumphant.

"She can't do it. She wants to be queen, but she still flinches at blood. This is where it ends."

She slid a small note across the table.

"Deliver this to Vega."

The note read:

"She hesitated. I won't. One queen. One kingdom."

At midnight, Callie was lying in wait on the rooftop of a parking garage in downtown Atlanta. Her breath fogged in the night air as she stood watching Zaire Monroe from a short distance. He was pacing near his car, talking on the phone, unaware of how close death was.

She had the silencer in her coat. The timing. The exit route.

And yet... she couldn't pull the trigger.

Her finger hovered. Her thoughts raced.

Was she really about to become this? Was she really about to cross the line she'd fought so hard to rise above?

And in that moment—Lila struck.

Police sirens echoed in the distance.

Someone had tipped off the authorities. Surveillance had been triggered. Zaire's security detail rounded the corner.

""GO!" Nova screamed through the earpiece. "Abort! It's a setup!"

Callie ran.

But in the distance, in her mind she could almost hear Lila's laugh.

Hours later, Callie stood in Emilio's war room at his estate, bloody knuckles, bruised pride, and failure hanging off her like smoke.

Emilio poured himself a drink slowly.

"She's winning," Callie said. "Lila made the call. The cops were waiting. My moment's gone."

Emilio said nothing for a few seconds. Then he nodded to his lieutenant, who left the room silently.

"You had one job," Emilio said coolly. "And you hesitated."

Callie clenched her fists. "You want loyalty? I'll prove it."

He raised an eyebrow.

"How?"

Callie stepped forward, pulled out her phone, and tapped a button.

A grainy video feed flickered to life on the screen beside them—Zaire Monroe, duct-taped to a chair in a soundproof room, eyes wide with fear.

"Lila was right," Callie said. "I did flinch. But I came back."

She looked up, eyes dark and certain.

"And this time—I didn't miss."

By the end of the week, Callie was standing next to Emilio Vega, now his right hand as cartel generals and political players filled the room. No longer a desperate survivor—now a partner in power.

Zaire Monroe was gone. The message was clear. Callie wasn't soft. She wasn't scared. And she sure as hell wasn't done.

Emilio raised his glass in front of the room. "Claymore Industries has my full protection," he declared. "Anyone who moves against Callie Morgan moves against me."

Applause followed. But behind the veil of smiles, Callie's mind was still working. Always.

As the crowd dispersed, Emilio leaned toward her. "The street trusts you now. But loyalty needs teeth. Build your core. Keep your enemies close."

Callie nodded. "Already working on it."

A few days later, Nova was in the private lounge at Claymore Industries. She opened the door to the sound of boots. Razor stepped in, bruised but alive—dark shades, a stitched brow, and a quiet fire in her eyes.

Briggs stiffened. "You got nerve showing your face here."

Callie stepped out from the shadows, calm as ever.

"I sent for her," she said.

Nova blinked. "After what she did?"

"She did what Lila told her to," Callie replied. "Now she's going to do what I tell her to."

Razor removed her shades. "I'm not loyal to ghosts. Lila left me to die. You giving me a lifeline."

Callie smirked. "Then welcome to Claymore."

Fulton County Jail – Lila's Cell

A guard approached her slowly, a folded note in hand.

Lila took it calmly, unfolded it.

Two words.

Too late

Her jaw clenched. She stood quickly.

Another guard was already approaching.

"Your outside line's been cut," he said. "Orders from Vega himself."

Lila's eyes narrowed.

For the first time in years—Lila felt checkmated.

Chapter Ten

Power Never Sleeps

Cartier closed the blinds in his office, the news replaying footage of Callie shaking hands with top civic leaders at a new Claymore redevelopment site.

"Just a few months back, Callie was DOA in the business world. Now, unbelievably, she's capturing everyone's admiration," Serenity remarked, shaking her head with her arms crossed. "And locking down the streets."

"She's got Vega behind her. That changes

everything," Cartier added. "And Razor's back in play. Lethal combination."

Serenity turned. "We've been too quiet."

Cartier nodded. "We attempted to rise above the chaos. Business as usual. Let the battles play out without getting involved. But this war's coming for us whether we're ready or not."

Serenity's voice was low. "In that case, we should prepare."

Fulton County Jail – Visitor Wing

Lila sat motionless at the metal table, wrists cuffed, back straight.

Callie entered in all black, a luxury coat thrown over her shoulders like a cape. She didn't sit.

"I wanted to see the look on your face when you realized I won," Callie said, smug. "Zaire's gone. Vega's backing me. Razor's with me now. You? You've got time."

Lila's face didn't change. Not a blink. Not a flinch.

"I should thank you," Callie added. "Without you, I wouldn't be this dangerous."

She turned to leave, smiling.

But Lila's voice stopped her cold.

"I'm not done yet."

Callie turned slowly.

Lila's eyes finally met hers—sharp, calm, chilling.

"You'll live to regret showing up here to gloat. This is not the end, you've only claimed the surface. The foundation is still mine."

Callie narrowed her eyes. "You're bluffing."

Lila leaned forward slightly. "Keep telling yourself that. It makes watching your downfall that much sweeter."

Callie sat across from Emilio, the room thick with cigar smoke and the sharp scent of old power. Emilio's gaze was calculating, as always, but today there was something sharper in his eyes—a recognition of the risks Callie had taken, and perhaps a reminder of the price she still had to pay.

"You've moved fast, Callie," Emilio said, swirling his drink slowly, his tone more neutral than approving. "Claymore is expanding, the city's top officials are falling in line, and you've made all the right moves to secure the streets. But this isn't a charity. As I told you before, loyalty has a price, and I don't need a partner who forgets that."

Callie clenched her jaw, yet her expression revealed nothing. The weight of Emilio's words hung heavy in the air. She had made deals, built alliances, and solidified her position, but in no way was this her end game. Emilio was a dangerous ally—and an even more dangerous enemy, so Callie knew she had to move with caution.

"I haven't forgotten, Emilio. I'm aware of the price," she said, her tone staunch. "I'm not just building Claymore for the streets. I'm building it for something bigger. I have a vision."

Emilio placed his drink aside and leaned in. "I've seen ambition before, Callie. But ambition alone doesn't build empires. You need more than muscle and money. You need control, and you need loyalty."

Callie reflected on how loyal she'd been to Cartier. Her mind flashed to his face, his touch, the passion they once shared. She could still feel the pull between them, even after everything had happened. Serenity was now the woman by his side, the one who had stood by him when the world turned against him. But Callie knew she was the one who truly understood him.

She wasn't just building an empire. Callie was building a legacy—a legacy Cartier would respect, maybe even admire, someday.

"Trust me, Emilio. I know the importance of loyalty, and I'll have that," she said, her voice hardening, the raw edge of emotion masked by steel resolve. "I'll have both."

Later that night, Callie stood alone in the sleek, glass-walled lounge overlooking the city. The lights of Atlanta twinkled like diamonds beneath her, a city full of possibility, but Callie knew better than anyone how fragile everything could be.

She had it all—almost. Emilio's protection, the city's resources, but what she really wanted—what she needed—was Cartier.

Her thoughts flickered to him. The way he had looked at her once, like she was the only thing that mattered. The passion they shared—the way they fed off each other's ambition and drive. Callie had always known that what they had was rare. She couldn't let Serenity, the quiet, composed woman with no understanding of the game, take him from her.

Cartier required someone who understood the darkness he fought against. Serenity couldn't give him that. She was too pure, too safe. Callie was the storm he needed, the power he craved.

She knew what she had to do—what she would do—to make Cartier see her as the one who could stand beside him, not just as a lover but as an equal, a partner who would never bail when the stakes were at their highest.

"I'll show him what power looks like. I'll make him realize I'm the only woman who can match him," Callie stated, determined to speak it into existence.

Chapter Eleven

Love On The Brain

The day after the announcement of Claymore's latest expansion, Callie found herself in the lobby of CR Enterprises. She hadn't seen Cartier in months, but today, the weight of her feelings felt too heavy to ignore.

She had come to prove something—to herself and to him. She stepped off the elevator, her heels clicking sharply on the marble floors. The receptionist barely glanced up as she approached Cartier's office door, but Callie didn't care. She wasn't here for pleasantries. She wasn't here to be polite.

She knocked once, and the door opened without a word. Cartier stood inside, his back to her, the skyline of the city transformed into a moody mural by the storm. Rain lashed against the glass like the world intended to breach his private refuge. She could see the tension in his posture, the way his shoulders were taut, like he was carrying a weight just like she was.

"Callie," he said, turning slowly, his face a mix of surprise and wariness. He stood tall and confident; his impeccable designer suit perfectly tailored to accentuate his muscular frame. His dark hair was immaculately cut, and his chiseled features exuded a sense of power and wealth.

Callie stepped inside; her gaze unflinching. She had nothing to hide anymore. Nothing to lose.

"I wanted to see you, Cartier," she said softly, but her words were sharp, filled with everything that had been building up inside her. "I know you've moved on. I know you've chosen Serenity. But I can't stand by and let her have the life we should be sharing together."

Cartier's face softened, but only for a moment. "Callie, we've been through this. What we had—it wasn't enough. You can't keep coming back to this."

"But it is enough," she snapped. "You think she's the one who can stand with you when the world is crumbling? She doesn't get this. She doesn't get you. I'm the only one who does. You and I—we understand what it takes to survive, to build something that lasts. I'm not asking for you to love me. I'm asking you to see that I'm the one who knows what it takes to win."

She moved closer, her voice filled with urgency. "I'm not asking for your forgiveness, Cartier. I'm asking for your respect. And I will earn it, in ways Serenity never will."

The tension in the room was palpable. Callie's eyes remained fixed on Cartier as he looked away. He'd changed—time had a way of doing that. The man she once knew had evolved.

"I know you remember what we shared—what we built together—it wasn't some fleeting moment. It was real."

Cartier's gaze softened, but only slightly. His eyes betrayed no real warmth, only the quiet, calculated man he still was.

"You know, Callie, you're right. We did build something. But you and I... we were different people back then." His voice was low, almost distant, as he walked closer to the window, staring out at the city. "I was married to Lila. I thought I could love both of you—thought I could keep it all separate. But you and I both know I was fooling myself. I wasn't the man I am now. You know that better than anyone."

Callie's eyes flashed with emotion, but she kept her composure. She didn't back down. She couldn't afford to.

"You're right," she said, her voice tight with the weight of their shared history. "You were married to Lila when we began our relationship. But I stood by you, Cartier. I went to prison because of my love and loyalty to you. I stood trial and was willing to take the fall for you. I loved you then, and I still do."

"That might be true, Callie. But it wasn't you who got us out of that bullshit Lila orchestrated. It was Serenity." His voice was blunt, but it was the truth. "She's the one who found the evidence, the one who proved we were innocent. You were loyal, but it was Serenity who did the work. She was the one who kept us from prison."

The sting of his words landed harder than Callie expected. But she refused to show weakness.

"I don't need you to remind me what Serenity did for us," she said quietly. "I'm not here to discuss her. I'm here to remind you what we meant to each other—and what I'm willing to do to make sure it's not over. I'm building Claymore to be a powerhouse, to prove to you that I'm the woman you should be with. Not her."

Cartier's expression shifted, though there was no anger in it—just a calm finality. He didn't meet her gaze right away, but when he did, his words were measured, almost tender.

"I wish you well with Claymore, Callie. You've built something impressive. But you need to be careful. Emilio Vega... he's not someone to trifle with. You know that. His protection comes with strings, and I know you're no stranger to that kind of deal." His voice darkened slightly, a shadow crossing his features as he spoke of the cartel.

"I'll handle Emilio," she said coolly. "I'm not a stranger to power. I've made deals of my own separate from him. Emilio is for the moment. My future is with you."

Cartier stepped closer; his voice more intimate. His eyes locked with hers, and for a moment, the past seemed to stretch between them—both of them remembering what they once shared.

"My future is with Serenity," he stated firmly, his words cutting through the air like a blade.

"She's going to be my wife. She's the one I'm building a life with. I'm sorry, Callie, but that's the truth. I'm not the man I was with you. I've moved on."

Callie stood frozen for a moment, her mind racing. He was choosing her. Serenity. The woman who hadn't shared the same darkness, hadn't fought the same battles. The woman who didn't know how to survive in a world like theirs.

"I see," Callie said, her voice barely above a whisper, but with an underlying promise in her tone. "I see how it is."

She kept her composure, even as a storm of emotions raged inside her. She would not beg. She would not plead. She had done enough of that already.

"I'm not giving up on you, Cartier," she said, her eyes burning with a quiet, fierce determination. "I'll make you see that I'm the woman you should be with. Not her."

For a long moment, Cartier didn't say anything. His eyes softened, but he stood firm.

"I hope you find what you're looking for. But it won't be with me."

Callie nodded slowly, turning toward the door, her heart heavy with the weight of his words. But as she reached for the handle, she turned back one last time.

"I'll get you back," she said softly, but with certainty. "I'll make you realize I'm the one you need."

As she exited the office, the door closed with a soft click. Her thoughts were already focused on the actions she needed to take next. Callie was committed to her decision, and now she was determined to ensure Cartier, and the world took notice.

Chapter Twelve

Crossing The Line

The room was softly lit, filled with the gentle hum of technology and the crisp aroma of freshly brewed coffee. Callie stood at the head of the table, her fingers tracing the map of the city sprawled across the screen. The markers on the map were a visual representation of Claymore's growth, but Callie's mind was elsewhere. Her thoughts were on Cartier. She couldn't lose him—not again. She had already sacrificed too much.

Nova and Briggs were present, as always, their loyalty solidified. They understood the stakes, but neither of them could fully grasp what Callie was about to do.

"No more playing small," Callie said, breaking the silence. "We've been focusing on expansion, building the empire. But once I acquire this major acquisition, Cartier will understand that I'm the one he should be with."

Briggs exchanged a look with Nova before responding. "We've secured the streets, Callie. You've made your mark. So, what is this major acquisition really about?"

Callie leaned forward, her eyes burning with intensity. "It's about showing Cartier that I'm not just a part of his past. I'm his future. When the dust settles, they'll be no doubt that I'm the one who can stand beside him. Not Serenity."

Nova frowned. "And how do you plan on doing that? You've got Emilio behind you, and—"

Callie cut her off. "I don't just have Vega. I have established my own resources and connections."

Briggs looked at her, his voice cautious. "You're going to put everything on the line over your obsession with Cartier?"

Callie nodded. "Everything. But it's not only about Cartier. It's about proving that I'm not just a survivor. I'm a force. I don't bow to anyone. And when this is over, I'll have my empire, and I'll have him. I'll make sure of it."

Later on that day, Callie sat at her desk, staring at the new contract in front of her. It was bold—dangerous even—but it was the kind of move that would solidify Claymore's dominance. If she could pull it off, the entire media landscape of Atlanta would bend to her will. She had already secured the necessary players, but the real challenge was keeping it under the radar until the deal went through, which she was pushing to happen immediately.

Her phone buzzed with a message from Nova: **This isn't the deal you got clearance for. Be careful.**

Callie knew exactly what Nova meant. This wasn't what she'd agreed to with Emilio. But the time for asking for permission had passed. If she wanted to make her mark, she had to act now.

Cartier had already made his choice, she thought bitterly. Now it was her turn to show him what he's been missing.

She smirked, typing out a text on her phone: **Tell them to pull the trigger. We go public tomorrow.** Callie stood in front of the full-length mirror in her office ready to do a celebratory dance, but she decided to wait until the contract was signed, sealed and delivered.

Callie lounged on the marble terrace of her midtown high-rise, basking in the early morning sunlight. She wore a silk robe that clung to her frame, the hue a perfect match for the orange liqueur in her freshly poured mimosa. In her left hand, she delicately pinched the end of a buttery croissant, occasionally tearing off a bite and chasing it with a sip of sparkling citrus. The city below was already stirring, the hum of traffic and distant sirens rising up through the crisp air, but up here, Callie felt insulated in a sanctuary of expensive glass and morning calm.

She wanted to be in the comfort of her home when the news broke. The nervous energy that had been coiling in her chest for days was finally transmuting into a sense of anticipation. Callie adjusted the cuff of her robe, ran a manicured finger along the rim of her flute, and then leaned back, closing her eyes to better savor the moment.

The warmth on her face was rivaled only by the slow burn in her chest as she thought about the little bombshell that was about to drop—and the domino effect it would set off. She could almost picture how the tight circle of power in this city would ripple and tremble when the secret finally detonated.

Claymore's new deal, which Callie had pushed forward without Emilio's clearance, was about to make major waves. A press release was scheduled to drop today, revealing her new business ventures and a partnership with some of the city's most influential people in media and politics.

But as the moment approached, things began to unravel. It started with a call from a number Callie didn't recognize.

"Hello," she said, trying to steady her breath.

"Callie, we have a problem," the voice on the other end said—it was one of the media moguls involved in the deal. "You didn't clear this with Emilio, did you? We've been getting calls from his people."

Callie's stomach dropped. She knew what this meant. "No, I didn't clear it. But the deal is already locked. We're going public."

"Not if we're going to stay alive in this city,"

the voice replied. "You better fix this, or we're pulling out."

Panic hit. The deal was about to blow up in her face. If Emilio found out, he'd see this as a direct challenge to his authority. Callie couldn't afford to lose this deal—not when it was the one thing that could put her on top.

Callie snapped into action. She picked up the phone and quickly called Nova and Briggs.

"I need you to get to City Hall, now!" she ordered. "We need to pull every string we've got. Get those signatures back in place, change the narrative, do whatever it takes."

Briggs's voice came through the phone, heavy with concern. "This is bigger than we thought. Emilio's going to find out, if he hasn't already."

"Don't care," Callie snapped. "Just fix it. We're not backing down."

She hung up, pacing back and forth on her terrace. Time was running out. The press release was only hours away, and Emilio's people were already sniffing around.

The next few hours felt like days. Callie didn't wait for Emilio's approval—she just moved. She fixed the media's narrative, convinced some key players to toe the line, and used her network to manipulate the story back into her control. By the time the press release dropped, she had successfully turned the tide—keeping her name in the game and the deal intact.

But, as expected, Emilio found out. Callie was summoned to his estate the next day. He sat in his office, reclining in his chair, his face betraying no emotion as he awaited her arrival.

"You know, I gave you a lot of freedom, Callie," Emilio began, his tone dangerously calm. "But what you did yesterday was reckless."

Callie swallowed, maintaining her poise. She knew what was coming.

"You didn't clear that deal with me," Emilio continued, his voice low, cutting. "You didn't even ask. You took matters into your own hands."

"I knew what I was doing," Callie said, her voice assertive. "The deal's secure. Everything is back on track."

Emilio's eyes narrowed. "That's not the point. You think you can operate like this without me? You think you can make moves and take risks without understanding that I'm the one who holds the power?"

Callie stood her ground, but there was no denying the weight of Emilio's words. She was a partner, but she wasn't in charge—not yet. She'd just overplayed her hand.

"I had to act, Emilio," she insisted. "I'm building something that's mine. And I need to prove I can do it on my own."

Emilio stood up slowly, walking around his desk. He stopped in front of her, towering over Callie with his imposing presence.

"You want to play with the big boys?" he said, his tone dark with warning. "Then you need to understand this. You're the face of Claymore, but I hold the power. You don't make moves like that ever again without coming to me first. Understood?"

Callie's jaw tightened, but she nodded. "Understood."

Emilio's gaze didn't soften. "Good. Now get to work. You've got more to prove."

Callie made her mark, but Emilio was the one pulling the strings. She wasn't the queen yet. She still had to play by his rules. But that didn't mean she would stop fighting for what she wanted. She would prove to Emilio, to everyone, that she could rise to the top on her own terms—no matter what it took.

Chapter Thirteen

Gold Veil, Glass Jaw

Serenity sat at a sleek table, gently swirling the wine in her glass while sifting through a pile of wedding planners. The room buzzed with quiet chatter, but her thoughts were miles away from the opulent setting of the restaurant. She was just beginning to plan her wedding with Cartier, yet the reality of creating a future together was proving more complex than she had anticipated.

The door swung open, and Donovan entered, his smile warm and sincere as he noticed her from across the room. He had become a consistent presence in her life ever since they collaborated to uncover the truth behind Lila's diabolical scheming. Despite the lingering awkwardness due to Callie's history with both of them, Donovan had always been open with her—a person she could trust.

"Hey there," Donovan said as he sat down across from Serenity. After ordering a drink from the waiter, he turned his focus back on her. "How's the wedding planning coming along?"

Serenity sighed and put her planner aside. "It's... overwhelming. There are so many things to consider, endless details. But Cartier has been absolutely amazing."

"Why wouldn't he be?" Donovan inquired.

"Perhaps it's my own assumptions. I figured since this is his second marriage, he wouldn't be interested in all the details. However, Cartier wants the wedding to be just as perfect as I do," she smiled.

Donovan's smile widened, with genuine warmth. "You deserve nothing less. After everything you've endured, the very least Cartier can do is ensure the wedding is exactly what you envision."

Serenity flashed him a quick smile before

she took a long, deliberate sip of wine. "I know. It's just difficult to focus on anything else with all this uncertainty looming over us."

Donovan's expression hardened slightly, his smile fading into a more serious, contemplative gaze. "I understand. I just want to make sure you're truly okay, amidst all this chaos."

"Honestly, Callie's constant power stunts are taking a toll," Serenity vented. "Cartier acts like CR Enterprises isn't being affected, but I can see he's concerned. How could he not be?"

Donovan paused briefly, glancing away before focusing back on her. "Look, Callie is one of my closest friends, and I work at Claymore too, but I disagree with how she's handling things. She's on a power trip."

"I'm not trying to make you betray your trust with Callie, because I understand how close you all are."

"Serenity, I appreciate that. But after everything we went through—getting Cartier and Callie out of prison and having the charges dismissed—we've grown close, and I count you as a dear friend too."

"Thank you, I feel the same way," Serenity

responded warmly. "That being said, isn't there a way for you to reach Callie? Whatever's driving her power trip, tell her to knock it off," she urged.

Donovan leaned back in his chair, a troubled expression clouding his features. He ran a hand through his hair, the tension evident in the crease of his brow.

"I've tried, Serenity. Believe me, I've tried," he admitted, frustration lacing his words. "It's like she's a different person since everything went down with Cartier. I can't get through to her like I used to. Honestly, I think he's a major influence on her actions."

Serenity tilted her head, curious. "What do you mean?"

"I believe Callie thinks that by proving she can dominate in the business world; she'll earn Cartier's respect, and he'll somehow realize she's the woman for him. It might sound unlikely, but to Callie, I think it's completely logical."

Serenity absorbed Donovan's words, her thoughts racing. The revelation about Callie's motives added a layer of complexity to the situation that she hadn't anticipated. She knew firsthand the lengths people would go to when driven by desire, power, or love.

"What do you think Callie is planning next?"

"I wish I knew, but I'm not certain. Briggs and Nova are the ones that have her ear. She promised me she wouldn't interfere with your relationship with Cartier, that she wouldn't disrupt your engagement. However, because of that promise, Callie withholds some things from me, things she knows I wouldn't approve of."

"So, in other words, Callie can't be trusted," Serenity shrugged.

"Callie's plotting something; I can sense it. Just stay vigilant. I'm always here for you, and I'll update you if I learn anything. Just don't lower your guard and be cautious."

Serenity sensed the tension hanging in the air and nodded slowly. She trusted Donovan, yet she was also aware of how dangerous Callie could be when she wanted something. It wasn't merely about gaining respect from Cartier—it was about something deeper, something more perilous that Callie harbored within her, and it could jeopardize all their lives.

In her office, Callie was reviewing the finalized

contract that secured the profitable deal she had closed on her own. Yet, despite this victory, she still found herself under Emilio's control.

Callie's attention snapped to Razor as she strode into the room, an unspoken understanding; there was no need for formalities. "You've been awfully quiet," Callie observed, her keen gaze tracking Razor as she settled into the chair across from her.

Razor reclined slightly, a defiant spark igniting in her eyes. "I've been staying under the radar, but I'm tired of it. I'm sick of Emilio's leash."

Callie leaned in closer, her voice charged with ambition. "I'm with you. I don't need Emilio anymore. I'm building my own empire, but first, we need to flip the power dynamic. I want to command the streets and those lurking in the shadows—not just the politicians and businessmen."

Razor nodded. "I get it. We need to form alliances with the other criminals, the key players—the ones who truly control the underground."

"Exactly," Callie shot back, her intensity sharpening like a blade. "We can't keep depending on Emilio for protection. He's just a steppingstone. My goal is total control. I want to dominate everything. But I need the right people with me.

I want to be the one making decisions, not just a pawn for him."

Razor leaned forward, "You know I have contacts. We have our networks. But you need enforcers. Those who don't just take orders—they push shit forward."

"Muscle is just a piece of the puzzle. We need influence—those politicians who've sold their souls, corrupt officials, and the underworld players who think they can straddle both sides of the fence. I'll give them what Emilio can't: a real seat at the table. We'll dismantle him from within."

Razor's grin widened, an eager spark igniting her eyes. "And then? We wipe out the competition?"

"Most definitely. This game isn't merely about cash; it's about wielding power. With the right players in our corner, I won't ever have to rely on Emilio again. We'll forge our own paths, and I'll be untouchable."

Razor sprang to her feet. "Let's make it happen then! Time to pull strings and execute our plan. I know people who will listen—but we have to be careful. Emilio's reach is long."

Callie rose with authority, striding toward the window where the city sprawled beneath her like a chessboard ready for conquest. "I'm aware of that. But he's not the only who can navigate this game—I'll outwit him."

Turning back to Razor, her voice was resolute and fierce. "We start recruiting our allies now—quietly and strategically. Soon enough, Emilio won't even see it coming."

Razor nodded sharply, determination mirroring Callie's own urgency. "Consider it done."

As Razor exited, Callie's mind surged with a torrent of possibilities. It was time to shatter the chains of Emilio's constraints, beginning by rallying the cartels to support her because no one was going to stop her.

Chapter Fourteen

No Mercy

Days had blurred together since Callie shared her plans with Razor. Now she needed to struck deals. Every move felt like a heartbeat, rapid and dangerous. Callie's plan was simple: take down Emilio, piece by piece. Corrupt officials, underground brokers, criminals—she had her eyes on all of them, every player in the game. But she couldn't let anyone see her hand. Not yet.

In the back of an upscale bar, the air thick with tension and the sharp scent of whiskey, Callie leaned against the polished mahogany. The soft hum of the city outside barely reached her ears, her focus all on the door. Diego walked in, his steps cautious, measured, like he was already anticipating danger. Good. He should.

"Diego," she said, voice smooth, eyes never leaving his. She was ready for this.

He eyed her with suspicion, arms crossed over his chest. "What's this about? Emilio won't like me meeting you."

Callie's lips curved into a cold smile. "Emilio doesn't own you," she said, stepping closer, the words like a warning shot. "You're not his puppet. You're just too scared to admit it."

Diego didn't flinch. He didn't look away. But she could see it—the crack in his loyalty. The shift in the way he stood, like he was already considering her words.

"I know Emilio," he said, voice low, "and he's not someone you just walk away from."

She leaned in, voice dropping even lower, the weight of her words carrying the promise of something bigger. "You think Emilio's untouchable? You're wrong. He's losing control. His empire's crumbling, Diego. You can keep clinging to him, or you can take what's yours."

His eyes flickered. A hint of doubt, barely there, but it was enough.

"What do you offer that he doesn't?"

"Freedom," Callie said, letting the word sink in. "No more orders. No more games. You take what's yours. You run your own operations, make your own decisions. You don't answer to anyone but yourself."

Diego's jaw tightened, but she could see the wheels turning. He was close. He could taste it.

"You think you can take him down?" he asked, still testing her, still holding back.

"I know I can," she snapped, the fire in her eyes cutting through the silence between them. "Together, we burn it all down. Inside out. You'll have loyalty from the ones Emilio's forgotten. The ones he's used, the ones he's left behind. The real power."

Diego's gaze shifted, his walls cracking just enough for her to see the ambition in his eyes. A dangerous, hungry thing.

"Think about it," she pressed, her voice hard, the promise of victory hanging in the air like smoke. "With me, you'll be unstoppable. Emilio won't even see it coming until it's too late."

For a second, he hesitated—just long enough for Callie to know she had him.

"All right," Diego said finally, voice cold as steel. "I'm in."

Callie's smile was slow, calculated, as she took a step back. "Smart choice."

They started talking plans, moving fast. Every word she said felt like a step closer to victory. For now, she would allow Emilio to think he's still got control. But the clock was ticking; and before long, they would attack when Emilio least expected it.

Emilio was an imposing figure, his posture regal exuding authority in custom tailored suits, his dark hair slicked back, yet his eyes bore the burden of his own influence. The rum swirled in his glass, a dark pool reflecting the decadent landscape outside his window. He surveyed his kingdom of lush gardens and sprawling grounds, a testament to his power and wealth. It was as if he were the ruler of a forgotten empire, a king surrounded by his riches yet unable to escape the creeping feeling of unease.

He was well aware of Callie's growing influence. It had taken time, but she was carving out a territory that now threatened his authority. He knew the game she was playing—he had seen it a hundred times before. But little did he know, his carefully cultivated empire was about to crumble at the hands of an ambitious adversary plotting against him, as Callie was more dangerous than most.

He picked up the phone and dialed a number he rarely called.

"Gather all the information you can on Callie Morgan," he instructed once the call was connected. "I need a detailed account of her activities over the past week—everyone she's meeting and talking to. I'll deal with this personally."

As the line went dead, Emilio shifted slightly in his chair, the soft leather creaking beneath him, his fingers tapping slowly on the armrest. He had trusted Callie—let her get too comfortable under his protection. But now, she was testing him, and it wouldn't be long before she had to pay the price for underestimating the depth of his control.

Chapter Fifteen

The Cost of Ambition

Callie had officially fast tracked her takedown of Emilio. She sat alone at a table in a dark, forgotten warehouse on the edge of the city. Shadows clung to every corner, making it the perfect place for business that needed to stay in the dark. Razor stood across from her, flanked by two men—silent, dangerous brokers with their fingers on the pulse of the streets, each one a link in a chain she was building.

"I've got something for you," one of the brokers said, sliding a thick file across the table. "A list. City officials—deep in the game with the competition. Bribed. Bought. They're already manipulating the system, playing both sides. We can use them, but we'll need leverage."

Callie opened the file, her fingers flipping through the pages. Names. Faces. Positions of power—all tied to Emilio's downfall. Each name was a potential ally, a key in the lock she was about to break open. The pieces were falling into place, one by one, and with every name she checked off, she could feel the walls around Emilio starting to crack.

"These guys aren't loyal to anyone but their own greed," Callie muttered, her eyes scanning the list. "And that makes them mine. I want them all. Every single one of them. But we play it smart—slow, careful. We won't leave a trace. We'll use Emilio's own weaknesses against him."

Razor nodded, in agreement. She understood the assignment. This wasn't just a business move—it was a war. And Callie was assembling an army.

"We'll make contact," the broker informed Callie. "You'll have them on your side before Emilio realizes he is no longer king."

Callie's smile was small, but deadly. "Good. Get it done."

The broker handed her a phone, already dialed to a number she needed. Callie took it, her grip firm as she placed it to her ear. "Start with the mayor," she said quietly. "Then the others. One by one. And don't leave anything to chance."

As the call connected, she glanced down at the list again. Each name was a thread in her web, guaranteeing she would be the one who stood at the top.

Razor's voice broke her focus. "What about the cartel members? We need more than just Diego."

She flipped open another folder, one filled with names of the cartel's inner circle. It was time to start checking them off too. She scanned the pages, calculating.

"Next step," Callie said, her voice low and lethal, "is the cartel. I want every name on this list turned. If they're not with us, they're against us."

She slid the folder across the table to Razor, eyes flashing with purpose. "Make it happen. I want them in line, or I want them gone."

Callie was engaged in combat, and the foremost principle of warfare was clear—show no mercy and take no prisoners.

Mastermind 3...

The weight of the decision was settling heavily on Callie's shoulders. She had been moving pieces around for weeks, setting up alliances with underground criminals, politicians, and media moguls. Yet, with every success, the pressure only mounted. Emilio was more aware of her moves than she would have liked.

It was only a matter of time, that he would trounce the gavel down on her, but Callie wasn't going to let him regain control. She had outmaneuvered him before, and she was confident she could do it once more.

The sound of a knock broke her thoughts. Nova entered, looking serious, her brows furrowed with concern.

"We've got a problem," Nova announced. "Emilio's men are sniffing around. They've traced our moves to some of the higher-ups we've been in contact with. We need to pull back, or he will go full nuclear."

Callie stood up from her desk, walking toward the window. She watched the city below, as if the answers she needed were hidden somewhere in the skyline.

"No," Callie said, her voice firm. "We keep going. I'll handle it. You've been doing well with the underground network. Make sure we don't leave any traces."

"Understood. But you know this will get ugly. Emilio is already making strategic moves to strip us of support. If we're not careful, we'll lose everything."

"That's why we strike first. We have one shot at this. Emilio thinks he has me cornered. He's wrong. I'll erase the weak links and expose them before he gets a chance to. We make the narrative ours."

"Are you sure that plan will work?" Nova wasn't convinced.

Callie nodded. "He's distracted. He thinks I'm just reacting, making small moves, but I'm setting up the big play. I've been working on something much bigger. We hit him hard enough, and the only option Emilio will have left, is to beg me for a seat at the table."

Nova had learned never to underestimate Callie. She had come back from the brink more times than she could count.

"We need to pick up the pace," Nova finally remarked.

"How are you progressing with the financials?" Callie inquired.

"Nearly ready to dismantle them."

"Excellent. Once we disrupt his financials, his entire operation will begin to collapse. That will cripple his supply chain and hit the cartel financially. Then the world will witness how fragile Emilio's empire is without his supporters."

Nova's eyes shone with approval. "That's a solid strategy."

Callie glanced over at her, eyes blazing with determination. "If we execute this properly, I won't just take Claymore—I'll take everything Emilio has built."

Chapter Sixteen

Desire and Dominion

The room was bathed in soft, golden light, the sun peeking through the curtains as Callie lay in the bed, her body languid and relaxed after the intense sex session. The man lying next to her—powerful, calm, and ruthless—shifted in bed, his hand gently brushing against her skin.

He was tall, with commanding, sharp features and a sleek precision of a fade, complimented with the natural allure of textured curls. To the world, his name held no significance, but to Callie, he was crucial to her scheme. He had been discreetly assisting her in devising strategies to weaken Emilio's influence.

"How do you always know exactly what I need," Callie murmured, turning over and kissing Gavion's chest.

"That's easy, we need the same thing." His voice deep and low, a smirk tugging at the corner of his lips.

Callie reclined against the pillows, a satisfied smile gracing her lips as she met his gaze.

"You're right, it explains why no one pleasures me like you do," she purred, her tone silky but edged with the quiet authority she'd honed over the years.

He reached over, threading his fingers through her hair and studying her features. "So, what's next on your agenda, Callie?"

She tilted her head, brushing a strand of hair aside. "You mean ours. Every step I've taken so far has been under your guidance."

He tittered. "And you've been an exceptional student."

"I have," she agreed with equal playfulness. "After taking down Emilio, I'll graduate at the top of the class."

He smiled. "Perfect protégé. There's so much more I want to teach you."

Gavion's words echoed in her ears, but Callie's mind drifted back to when Cartier claimed her as his protege. She stared at the ceiling, nodding as if listening, yet replaying in her mind the hidden maneuvers she'd orchestrated—planting key players, corrupt officials, media titans—and, most of all, Cartier himself. And yet, even with Gavion beside her, her heart ached for Cartier.

Her fingers tightened on the sheets, she remembered the empty space he'd left, how Serenity had smoothly taken her place. The sting of being cast aside cut deep, but Callie vowed it wouldn't last.

She blinked, refocusing on Gavion. "You've taught me that Emilio isn't invincible. I now have everything to bring him down, and I'm positioned to move boldly. His empire stands on fragile alliances. One decisive strike, and it all collapses."

Gavion raised an eyebrow. "And Cartier? You keep him hovering on the edges of your scheme. But word is he's a different man now that he's with Serenity. His loyalty is pledged to her. What's your play for that?"

Callie's pulse quickened. "Cartier's loyalty always belonged to power," she said softly, knowing she desperately wanted him back by her side. "Once I seize control, he'll have no choice but to align with me. Together, we'd be an unstoppable force this city couldn't touch."

"In business, pleasure, or both?" he prodded.

"Business, of course," she replied. "I have no desire to return to Cartier's bed. I've moved on from him in every way besides business," Callie lied.

"Seems you have it all figured out."

She turned to face him fully, eyes locked on his. "I do. When Emilio falls, I will control everything. Claymore will be mine, and I'll prove to the world I'm not just another player—I am the game itself."

Gavion's expression was inscrutable. "You're clearly enjoying this dangerous dance. But be careful. Sometimes the hunter gets captured by the game," he warned.

Emilio sat in his dark office, staring at the file in front of him. Callie's recent moves had pushed the boundaries of his patience, but she wasn't the only one playing this game. He had allies of his own—men and women who owed him their loyalty and who would help him remove her from the equation if it came to that.

His phone buzzed. It was a text from one of his trusted informants: ***Just got the report. Callie's made a move on the media moguls. She's targeting city officials who are involved in her dealings and looking into your finances.***

Emilio immediately picked up the phone and called his informant. He sat back in his chair, fingers tapping the armrest as he listened to his report. "Callie Morgan is starting to hit your pockets, Emilio. She's cutting off some of your suppliers and moving in on the politicians who've been controlling the flow of money."

Emilio's eyes narrowed. "She thinks she can push me, and I won't retaliate?" his voice grew dark. "It's time I send a message—Callie needs to be reminded of her place and who holds the power." Emilio stated, his tone cold and commanding.

Emilio knew Callie was ambitious—an ambition that bordered on recklessness. She dared to think she could carve her own path, a dangerous dance with flames that threatened to consume her. But Emilio wasn't finished yet, and this tumultuous game was far from over.

Chapter Seventeen

Calm Before The Storm

The city below gleamed like a diamond, lights reflecting off the glass windows of Callie's office. The weight of the night's silence felt heavy, but Callie wasn't content to let the world rest. It was her moment—her empire was close to taking shape, but she knew the foundation could crumble at any moment if she didn't act with meticulousness.

She stood in front of her desk, the digital map of the city laid out on her screen. Every red pin, every marked location represented someone she controlled, someone she needed to keep in her pocket. The web she had woven was intricate, with Emilio's men and cartel informants scattered across it, but she needed more—more power, more leverage.

A knock at the door interrupted her thoughts.

"Come in," she called, not turning around.

Briggs stepped inside; his expression grim but focused. "We've been tracking Emilio's moves. He's starting to push back harder. He's pulling strings with some of the city's biggest players, trying to cut you off at the source."

Callie didn't flinch. She expected this. "Let him play his cards. I'll play mine."

Briggs glanced at the map on her desk. "Okay, but what's the approach?"

"I'm not going to wait for him to corner me," Callie said with certainty. "We've already penetrated Emilio's financial infrastructure, so he's vulnerable there—his remaining assets are tied to people who can be swayed. We target each one individually, and those who refuse to comply will soon regret ever aligning with him."

Briggs hesitated. "And when Emilio finds out?"

Callie gave a chilly and strategic grin that

revealed how far she was willing to go. "By the time he figures out what I'm doing, it'll be too late. We'll have the full support of the city's top business players, political leaders and the cartel members."

Briggs crossed his arms. "Can you offer more details on how exactly we are going to accomplish that?"

"They're nervous about Emilio's instability. I'm going to offer them a better deal—Claymore's deal. We cut off Emilio's remaining suppliers, turn them into allies, and make him look weak."

"That can work for the city's business and political leaders, but Emilio's cartel ties run deep. He won't back down quietly."

Callie's eyes flashed with determination. "I'm not expecting him to. But that's the beauty of it. We'll make him think he's winning, right up until the moment his entire world collapses."

Cartier stood up, his well-defined muscular frame cutting a striking silhouette against the expansive window, with the city skyline unfolding before him like a masterpiece. A breathtaking tapestry of glimmering lights and towering structures, each representing a piece of the empire he had meticulously crafted. And soon, the final piece, Serenity would be his wife, and they have the life they had always envisioned.

Just as he allowed himself a moment to savor this vision of success, his phone buzzed sharply on the sleek desk, the vibration snapping him back to reality. Cartier's eyes flicked to the screen. Seeing Spencer's name gave him pause, but he answered promptly.

"What's up Spencer? My day has been going wonderful so far. I hope this call doesn't alter that."

"You're gonna want to hear this," Spencer's voice crackled through the phone, low and heavy with something between urgency and concern. "I'm hearing things—Callie's problems with Emilio have escalated. You know they've been at odds for a minute, but now she's taking actions that might ignite a full-blown war."

Cartier paused, his posture shifting as he pushed off the window, eyes narrowing. "What kind of moves?"

Spencer's voice dropped even lower. "She's

made deals behind Emilio's back, playing both sides. Word is the cartel's backing her more openly. There's talk of her going rogue. And you know—when Callie's backed into a corner, she's dangerous."

Cartier's fingers dug into the edge of his desk, frustration creeping into his gut. Callie. Emilio. Two people from his past, engaging in the street mayhem he thought he'd left behind. Some of their business ventures would inevitably brush up against each other, but Cartier had no desire to get dragged into their war.

"I'll resolve this," he said, tone steady. "I've ensured CR Enterprises maintained legitimacy to avoid getting caught up in Callie's bullshit. We're staying far removed from this."

Spencer paused, like he was weighing something heavy. "You sure? You could use this situation to your advantage and make a power play."

Cartier shook his head, though Spencer couldn't see the movement. "Nah. I'm not getting wrapped up in Callie's chaos. We've got a wedding to plan, and Serenity deserves my full attention. This battle between Callie and Emilio? Not my fight."

There was a long pause on the other end of the line. Then Spencer spoke, using a more diplomatic tone. "I get it. But keep in mind, it's not just her shutting down Emilio. If Callie starts shaking things up on her own turf, it could bleed into yours. Just say the word if you want to move on it."

Cartier let out a slow breath, turning away from the window, the city sprawled out beneath him like an empire waiting to be claimed. "Continue to keep watch and just make sure we're ready, if we need to make a move. This is bigger than Callie's petty power plays. I won't let her screw up what I've built."

He hung up and stared out at the skyline once more. He was in a good place, finally. Serenity had been the one constant in his life, and now that they were planning their future together, he wouldn't let anything—or anyone—threaten it. Not Callie, not Emilio, and certainly not anyone who wanted to pull him back into the chaos.

As his thoughts lingered on Serenity, a slight smile tugged at the corner of his mouth. She was everything he had been waiting for, everything he needed. They had built something real, and he wasn't about to let that slip away.

Chapter Eighteen

Lethal Alliances

Callie was reviewing the latest intel on her expanding business empire, when a message popped up on her phone from one of her inside sources. It was from a trusted contact—someone she had keeping close tabs on Serenity and her wedding plans.

The message was short but revealing: **The wedding planner for Serenity and Cartier is Lisa McCall. Her business is small but it's also one of the most exclusive in the city.**

Callie's thoughts whirled. Serenity and Cartier's wedding was about to become a far more significant event than she had expected. She had been monitoring the situation, but upon discovering who the wedding planner was, she saw an opportunity to exploit this knowledge for her own benefit. This wasn't merely a wedding; it represented their future—a future Callie was resolute in sabotaging.

Her eyes danced as an idea began to form. She wasn't about to let Cartier's happiness go unchallenged.

She picked up the phone, dialing the number of one of her employees—someone she had been quietly pulling into her fold over the past few months. The call connected, and Callie's voice was direct and businesslike.

"I need you to do something for me. I want you to approach Lisa McCall. Get close. She's Serenity's wedding planner, and I need every detail about that wedding. From the guest list to the dress to the flowers, I want to know everything. Ensure she communicates with you. You'll serve as my eyes and ears from within."

Her employee responded quickly, "Understood, Callie. I'll get to work."

As she ended the call, a storm of thoughts

swirled in her mind. This wedding was going to be a disaster, and she was going to make sure Serenity and Cartier never reached the altar.

The prison walls were cold and unforgiving as Cartier stood before the metal bars separating him from Bradley Upton, his former second-in-command. The man who had once been his best friend. The betrayal that had been festering in Cartier's chest for months had come to a head, and now, standing in front of Bradley, Cartier could hardly contain the anger boiling inside him.

Bradley looked up from his bench as Cartier entered, his face stoic but with a trace of guilt hidden in his eyes. His jumpsuit clung to his broad shoulders, and his hands were clasped tightly in front of him. It had been a long time since they last spoke, and the silence between them now felt like a chasm.

Cartier folded his arms, his gaze steely. "I never thought I'd see you incarcerated. You were the sensible one to counter my darker impulses.

Yet, you chose to turn on me. You are a reminder, betrayal doesn't come from your enemies, only from those you trust to stand next to you."

Bradley didn't flinch. He had spent months thinking about this moment, and now that it was finally here, he had no defense. "I don't expect you to understand, Cartier. I was always in your shadow. The company—what you were building—it wasn't enough. Lila... she convinced me."

"Lila," Cartier scoffed, his voice harsh. "She's the reason you turned your back on me, so the two of you could plot behind my back, my wife and my best friend. You allowed Lila to destroy everything we had."

Bradley sighed heavily, looking down at the floor, his voice cracking slightly. "I didn't want to hurt you. I did consider you a friend. But I got gripped in Lila's web."

Cartier's fists clenched; the betrayal still too fresh in his mind. "You betrayed me. You took everything I built, everything I trusted, and handed it over to her. And for what? To be her lapdog?"

Bradley paused before replying, contemplating the significance of his actions. When he finally broke the silence, his voice was more deliberate. "I apologize. At first, I believed my actions were in the best interest of CR Enterprises, but then the lure of power overtook me."

Cartier shook his head in disbelief. "It was never about the greater good for you. It was always about power. You and Lila tried to bring me down, and now you're both behind bars with nothing but memories of the control you used to have."

Bradley's eyes met Cartier's, neither fully understanding the other's intentions. "There's more you need to know. You need to understand the dynamics between Lila, Callie, and Emilio. It's all connected. They share a history that is more intertwined than you realize—before Lila even met you."

Cartier's curiosity piqued. "What do you mean?"

Bradley leaned forward. "Lila and Callie were inseparable—like sisters—long before you appeared in their lives. They shared an unbreakable bond. But then you married Lila, and your relentless infidelity drove her to the brink. She sought out Callie to devise a plan to teach you a lesson and make you pay. But when Callie fell in love with you, Lila felt the sharp sting of betrayal, and that so-called lesson spiraled into a disaster none of us could foresee. And now, from what I heard, Callie has partnered with Emilio. That path is fraught with danger and will surely lead to ruin."

Cartier's thoughts were in overdrive. He had long suspected Callie had her own motives, but he never realized the extent of her ties to Lila and Emilio.

"I sensed there was more to their relationship," Cartier mumbled, mostly to himself rather than to Bradley. "But Emilio... how does he fit into all of this?"

Bradley's eyes showed a blend of fear and resignation. "Emilio was always lurking in the shadows. I know he's the one who rescued Claymore when Callie was about to lose everything. I'm certain Callie had to pay dearly for Emilio's assistance. But as you know, Callie craves power, and even Emilio can't control her. So, trouble is looming."

Cartier paused for a moment to absorb the information. "How do you have all this information?" he asked.

Bradley leaned back against the wall of his cell. "I was there," he replied. "I witnessed it all. Lila and Callie were conspiring to take you down, and Emilio... he's not just any business figure. He's the leader of a significant cartel with extensive influence."

Mastermind 3...

Cartier's mind was reeling. Callie, Lila, Emilio... The puzzle pieces were fitting together, and this revelation only intensified the conspiracy involving the two women he once trusted.

"Tell me everything about Emilio," Cartier demanded, his voice growing firm. "I need to know who his allies are, his connections—everything."

Bradley held his gaze, and after a long pause, he began, "I'll share what I can. But you must understand—going after Emilio isn't just business. It's a war, and you'll need more than just your company to take him on."

Chapter Nineteen

Ambush

Serenity walked through the venue, heels clicking against the polished marble. The place was a show-off's dream: chandelier after chandelier hanging from the high ceilings, their crystals catching the dim light just right. The walls were wrapped in sleek velvet, a deep red that screamed "luxury," and the floor gleamed like it had never seen a single misstep. It was almost too perfect. It felt like a set for a movie, too staged to feel real.

Mastermind 3...

Her wedding planner, Lisa McCall was a petite powerhouse in a designer suit who looked like she was fresh out of a high-end magazine, was talking her ear off about the space. "This ballroom is exactly what you need. It's grand, but not too much. Perfect for your ceremony," she said, voice airy yet professional.

Serenity nodded, pretending to listen, her mind already running through the details of her big day: Cartier at the end of the aisle, her dress, the vows—everything falling into place. Until the sound of footsteps behind her cut through her thoughts. She turned sharply, and there she was. Callie.

Standing in the doorway like a queen who had just seized a kingdom. The woman was pure chaos incarnate, and Serenity's heart plummeted at the mere sight of her.

"Callie," Serenity hissed, venom lacing every syllable. "What the hell are you doing here?"

Callie remained unfazed, her expression a mask of infuriating calm. "Just scoping out the competition," she replied, her voice dripping with an unsettling nonchalance that made Serenity's skin crawl. "This place has potential. Too bad it's all for nothing. Just a waste"

Serenity's heart pounded violently in her

chest, adrenaline surging. She knew exactly where this confrontation was headed. "The only waste is you showing up at this venue on some stalker shit," she retorted, fighting to keep the rising fury from cracking her voice.

Callie shrugged, her eyes sweeping the room as if she owned it. "Is that what you're thinking? That I'm a stalker?" she asked, her heels echoing with each step as she moved past Serenity, surveying everything as if she had a claim to it. "I'm insulted. I'm far more dangerous than that.

Serenity moved closer, narrowing the gap between them. "At this stage of my life, a little danger doesn't intimidate me. In fact, sometimes I even embrace it," she retorted, meeting Callie's gaze. "But surely you wouldn't put your life in danger for a man who's made it clear he doesn't want you?"

Callie halted and slowly turned around, a self-satisfied grin spreading across her face. "Honey, he's already decided, and it's definitely not you." She leaned in, her voice dropping to a menacing whisper. "I'm the one he desires. I'm the one he's meant to be with. You're just a diversion, a hurdle. And believe me, you'll never reach that altar."

"This ring on my finger tells a different story," she replied, lifting her hand to display the dazzling diamond. "You're delusional, Callie, and it doesn't suit you," Serenity mocked.

Callie's eyes blazed with a sinister glint that sent shivers down Serenity's spine. "A ring means nothing without an 'I Do'," she said, her voice low, edged with a menacing undertone. "You won't make it down that aisle as long as I'm around."

With a haughty turn, Callie walked away, exuding that same infuriating arrogance that made Serenity want to scream. The wedding planner shifted uncomfortably in the background, too shocked to speak.

Serenity glanced around the lavish venue once more, the gleaming chandeliers and velvet-covered walls suddenly feeling like a cage. This was supposed to be the start of the rest of her life with Cartier—the one thing she'd been fighting for—but now, it all felt uncertain. Callie's words reverberated in her mind, loud and unmistakable. Serenity sensed the heaviness of her threat lingering in the air, suffocating her like the room itself. And for the first time, she hesitated about walking down that aisle.

The moonlight was barely a whisper against the darkened streets of the industrial district. The safehouse, a once quiet hub for cartel operations, now felt like a ticking time bomb. Callie had been watching for weeks. The cartel member, Juan Delgado, had been one of the last to resist her offer—an alliance she had worked tirelessly to secure. But Juan had been stubborn. Arrogant. He refused to align with her against Emilio, believing he could continue playing both sides.

Now, Callie's patience had worn thin.

She stood in the shadows outside, her hand clasped around the cold grip of her phone. Her mind was sharp, calculating each move before it unfolded. The decision had been made—Juan had outlived his usefulness. And he would be removed from the board.

Razor, her trusted enforcer, was positioned a block away, eyes trained on the entrance to the building where Delgado and his crew were holed up. She was always ready for a fight—her icy calm in the midst of violence was something Callie had come to depend on.

Mastermind 3...

A quick message buzzed on Callie's phone: **Ready.** It was from Razor's team, stationed inside the building.

Callie exhaled, giving the order. "Let's make this clean."

Juan Delgado sat in a dusty chair, his legs stretched out, a glass of whiskey in hand. He was unaware that his empire—built on lies, deceit, and unstable alliances—was about to come crashing down. The room was faintly lit, the sound of murmured conversations around him drowned by the low hum of an old fan. His men were scattered, unprepared for what was coming.

Suddenly, the door swung open, and the sound of footsteps echoed through the hallway. It was too loud for a normal visit.

Juan looked up, noticing a dark figure near the door, and he roared. ***"¿Quién diablos eres?"***

Before he could say more, the door burst open, and two of Callie's men stormed in, guns raised. There was no time for questions, no time for a fight. Juan barely had time to react before a shot rang out, cutting the silence. His bodyguard was taken down in an instant.

"Juan Delgado," the first man spoke, his voice cold and firm. "Your time is up."

Juan's eyes widened in shock as he fumbled for his own weapon, but it was too late. The second enforcer moved swiftly, his gun pressing against Juan's temple as the others cleared the room.

"Callie said you'd be a problem," the enforcer whispered, his grip tight on Juan's arm. "Now we're cleaning up."

Callie stood motionless, watching through the camera feed as the scene unfolded. The surveillance inside the building gave her the exact view she needed—the first few shots had been enough to incapacitate the guards.

Razor's voice crackled over the speaker in her ear. "It's done. Delgado's been neutralized. The rest will follow. We're pulling out."

Callie smirked, "Good. The city's mine now."

This was the final strike in her effort to wrestle power away from Emilio. Juan's unwillingness to join her had cost him everything. And now, she controlled another key piece in the cartel's operation. This was a turning point.

She watched as the men dragged Delgado's body out of the safehouse, leaving no trace behind. No one would be able to link it to her. The cartel's dissenters were disappearing, one by one. Callie's dominance was growing, and soon,

Emilio would have no choice but to bow to her.

The music thumped in the background as Callie stood in front of the mirror, adjusting the silk black dress that clung to her curves. For a moment, she allowed herself to feel the rush—the feeling of victory, of control slipping from Emilio's fingers and into her own grasp. This was her moment. The night was hers. The city was about to realize that Callie Morgan was a force to be reckoned with, and anyone who doubted her would be swept aside. She had orchestrated the perfect ambush—Juan Delgado had been holding out and refusing to align with her, and now he'd been taken down. His blood was spilled on the streets, and his organization was ripe for the picking. She could feel the power shift in her favor. Emilio's grip on the city no longer existed.

She stepped out of her office, heading to the private lounge where a small, exclusive celebration was underway. Champagne flowed, and the room buzzed with people loyal to her—business moguls, underground players, and a few faces she had cultivated from the shadows.

"To Callie Morgan," one of her associates toasted, raising his glass.

The room echoed with applause as she lifted her own glass, smiling in her usual calculated way.

"To the future," she replied, her voice smooth and confident.

For a moment, she allowed herself to feel the rush—the feeling of triumph, of control slipping from Emilio's fingers and into her own grasp. This was her moment. The city was about to realize that Callie Morgan was a force to be reckoned with, and anyone who doubted her would be eliminated.

Cartier sat at his desk, a storm brewing in his mind. His attention shifted between the stacks of paperwork, his recent conversation with Bradley, and the latest events surrounding Callie's escalating power moves. Despite no longer sharing an intimate relationship, he knew professionally their paths crossed and that her relentless efforts to wrestle control away from Emilio would create chaos in the city. If Callie couldn't be controlled, it would be problematic with his own business affairs.

As he was becoming further engrossed in his thoughts, Cartier's phone buzzed with a message from Spencer: ***We've got intel that someone big is making moves against us. It's not just Callie and Emilio anymore. There's a third player***.

Cartier's heart sank as he read the message. A third player? He immediately began contacting his allies in the city to gather more information. He knew what this meant. This wasn't just a battle for control—it was a war, and if he didn't act quickly, he could lose it all.

Chapter Twenty

The Ultimatum

Callie's heart raced with anticipation as she and Razor made their way toward Emilio's estate. Juan's death was her victory, her final move to solidify her place at the top. With the cartel member out of the way, she now had enough leverage to confront Emilio directly. He would either bow down to her and acknowledge her rise or be removed from the equation permanently.

The mansion loomed ahead, its gates opening as they made their way inside. This would be Callie's final step solidifying her quest for full control. She had a plan, and she was ready to execute it. As she entered the grand hall, she found herself staring at a table where Emilio sat with a man beside him—a man Callie recognized immediately. Gavion. The lover who had been advising her on how to take down Emilio. Gavion's bodyguard stood nearby, his posture stiff.

But something was wrong. The atmosphere felt off. The man, whom Callie had trusted, was sitting next to her enemy, as if they were old friends. Callie's eyes narrowed in disbelief.

"What the fuck is this?" Callie asked, her voice icy, her anger starting to simmer.

Emilio looked up from his drink and smiled, his eyes glossy with a mixture of amusement and superiority. "Callie. I'm glad you could join us."

Her mind reeled. She took a step forward, Razor flanking her, but she was still in shock. "Answer me, Gavion. What in the hell are you doing here with Emilio?"

Gavion leaned back. "We've been discussing the future of the cartel."

"What about it?" her tone critical.

Emilio's chuckle filled the room as he looked at Callie with a patronizing smile. "You thought killing Juan Delgado was your ticket to power, didn't you? But all you did was eliminate one of the pieces on the board. You were never more than a pawn."

Callie's blood ran cold. She stood there, stunned, the truth dawning on her. The man she had trusted, the one she had believed was going to help her take down Emilio, had been playing her. He wasn't an ally. He was a part of Emilio's game.

"I thought you were helping me," Callie fumed, her fury boiling over. "I thought you wanted the same thing I did!"

Gavion shrugged nonchalantly, his cool demeanor unwavering. "I had to maintain control over the situation. You were never meant to lead."

Emilio raised his glass, looking directly at Callie. "You've been a valuable asset, Callie. But now, your usefulness has expired. I'll let you live, but you'll no longer be a partner. You'll be a worker, doing the dirty, heavy lifting while I remain the head of this cartel. It's my empire. And you're just a small piece of it." Emilio turned to Gavion full of bravado. "Isn't that, right?" he winked condescendingly.

Callie's chest tightened as her world crashed around her. She had been betrayed, outplayed, and now her life was at the mercy of men who saw her as nothing more than a tool.

Gavion nodded, seemingly agreeing with Emilio. But his gaze flickered to his bodyguard, and something shifted in the air. In a matter of seconds, before anyone could react, the room was filled with the sound of gunshots. Emilio's loyal guards dropped to the floor; their bodies lifeless before they hit the ground. Callie froze, her breath caught in her throat. She turned just in time to see Emilio's face distorted with fear as Gavion's bodyguard then shot him in the chest. Blood sprayed throughout the room, staining the marble floor. Emilio's eyes widened, and with one final, pained gasp, he collapsed to the ground.

Callie felt the wetness of Emilio's blood splattered across her face, and for a moment, she was paralyzed, her thoughts spiraling. Emilio was dead. The man who had held so much power—who had controlled everything—was now nothing more than a body at her feet.

She looked up, and Gavion was already standing. His expression remained unreadable, but there was a quiet satisfaction in his eyes. "Calm down, Callie. It's over for him. But not for you."

Callie's hands were trembling, her heart pounding in her chest. She had been so close to securing everything—power, control, and her place at the top. But now, everything was spiraling out of control.

Gavion stared at Callie, eyes calculating, as if the whole scene was nothing but a well-executed plan that had gone off without a hitch. She wiped the blood from her face, still in shock. Callie's eyes darted from Gavion to the bodyguard, then back to the entrance as the sound of footsteps echoed.

Another figure entered the room—an older man, walking with a quiet but commanding presence. Callie didn't recognize him, but there was something unmistakable about his demeanor. His aura was powerful—too powerful for someone so unknown to her.

Gavion turned towards the powerful figure to greet him. "Father," he said, his voice filled with respect.

Callie blinked in confusion. "Father? What—" She mouthed under her breath.

The older man's eyes met hers—sharp, shrewd. There was no warmth, no acknowledgment of her presence as a rival or ally, just an unspoken understanding.

"Father, this is the woman I told you about."

"You," the older man said, his voice low and

steady, "you've been playing a dangerous game, Callie. But it ends here."

Callie's pulse quickened. She glanced between Gavion and his father, still confused. The puzzle pieces were almost in place, but she couldn't put it together yet. Something was missing.

Gavion's cold smile only deepened, and he turned to his father, speaking in a voice barely above a whisper. "Should I tell her?"

His father placed his hand up, indicating he would take it from here. His piercing gaze locked with Callie's, and his voice carried an icy finality. "I am Cartier's father. And you, Callie, are nothing but a device in a much larger game."

Callie's throat tightened. Cartier Richardson, the one man she held close to her heart, her motivation for greatness, was part of the very family that had orchestrated her every move. Their presence meant all she had built was about to be ripped away. And the worst part was—she had never seen it coming.

Then Callie's eyes widened, and she felt a knot in her stomach. She turned to Gavion. "You're... you're Cartier's brother?"

Gavion nodded, his smile widening. "The one and only," he proudly stated.

Callie stood motionless, her breath shallow. The room felt too small, the walls closing in on her. She was caught in the web of a family she never even knew existed—Cartier's family. And now, she was at their mercy.

She glanced at Cartier's father—and then at his brother. This was no longer just about power. This was about survival. She had been bested in every meaningful way.

The father spoke again, his voice as cold as the steel of the barrel aimed at her. "I'm not here to play games. I've let you come this far, but you no longer have the luxury of choice. So, I suggest you think carefully." His soulless eyes fixed on Callie. "You can follow my lead, and live. But if you resist, you can die just like Emilio. The choice is yours."

Callie felt a spark of rage build within her—a mixture of betrayal and determination. The real game was now beginning because Callie refused to be anyone's puppet. But with the revelation that Cartier's father was the man behind everything—the mastermind, she was faced with a choice: bow down to this new power or accept her own demise.

Mastermind 3...

Coming Soon

Mastermind 4...

Cartier's War For The Throne

WWW.JOYDEJAKING.COM
@PRECIOUSCUMMINGSOFFICIAL

A KING PRODUCTION

Baller Bitches
VOLUME 1
PARTS 1-3

A NOVEL

JOY DEJA KING

Diamond

"Bitch, you ain't shit!" When my baby daddy stood in front of me screaming that bullshit with spit flying everywhere, I kept putting the clear coat of polish on my nails ignoring his ass. "Did you hear what the fuck I said?" he belted as the vein in the middle of his forehead started pulsating.

"Mutherfucka, everybody in the damn building can hear what the fuck you just said. Are you done ranting 'cause I got shit to do?"

"That's what's wrong wit yo' ass, yo' mouth too fuckin' slick."

"Umm this shit gettin' repetitive. Ain't but so many ways you can call me a bitch and tell me I ain't shit. I get it, you think I'm foul. So either come up with some new descriptions or move on to something else."

"I can't believe I got a baby wit' yo' stupid ass. You don't give a fuck about nobody but yourself. One day I promise I'ma take our daughter away from you because I refuse to let her grow up and end up like you."

I put my polish down and eyeballed Rico because I wanted him to know what I was about to say wasn't a game. "Nigga, the day you start plotting to take my daughter away from me is the day you better tell yo' mama to start making your funeral arrangements. You can call me every ho, dick sucker, no good bitch all mutherfuckin' day but when you bring Destiny into the mix we have a problem. Now please get the fuck out my crib and take that noise you spewing someplace else."

"Diamond, this shit ain't over. I'll be back tomorrow to pick up my daughter for the weekend and she better be here and not at your mother's house."

"I tell you what. Why don't you pick Destiny up from my mother's house tomorrow because I can't take having to see yo' ass two days in a row."

"No, I'll pick Destiny up from here tomorrow. So whatever partying and fucking you planning on doing tonight make sure you have yo' ass up in time to get my daughter in the morning."

"That's what your problem is now. So busy worrying about what the fuck I'm doing," I huffed under my breath not wanting to reignite the argument because I was ready for Rico to bounce.

"Bye," I said keeping my head down, until I heard the door shut.

There was a time an argument with Rico would fuck up my entire day but this shit had become so routine I barely broke a sweat over it now. See, there was a time when Rico was actually my boyfriend. I thought we would be together forever but that was when I was young and dumb. He swooped me up when I was fifteen and not used to good dick or money. When I was walking home from school one afternoon he pulled up in a tricked out Benz and I couldn't believe when he rolled down the window asking me for my name. He was one of those pretty niggas who knew his packaging was right.

From that day on we started dating. Rico would pick me up from school almost everyday and them chick's mouths dropped every time he pulled up and I would get in the car. We would go get something to eat and just talked. Although he was three years older than me he never made me feel like a kid instead I felt like a woman. But I wasn't a woman and Rico was way out of my league. He quickly made me his girl but that didn't keep him from having mad other bitches, so many I couldn't keep count. In the beginning I fell for all his lies. He had a valid excuse for every accusation I had. By the time I woke up to the truth it was two years later and I was pregnant with Destiny.

That was the roughest nine months of my life.

I had bitches calling my phone harassing me. They would say my man just left their crib and he fucked the shit out of them. My feet swelled up, belly poked out feeling depressed and helpless having to hear this shit. By this time, Rico wasn't even trying to hide his dirt anymore. He felt I was pregnant and stuck. Even after all that I stayed with Rico. It took another year before I wised up and gave that nigga the deuces. When I did, Rico tried to make my life a living hell. I guess he thought I would be a dumbass forever...not!

    I spent the first year of Destiny's life being with her day and night while Rico ran the streets. I don't even remember him changing one diaper. But I loved her so much it didn't even matter. Destiny was like my real life baby doll and she helped me get my shit together. I had gained so much weight during my pregnancy and even more afterwards and I think it was out of depression, because Rico had me so stressed out. I decided I had to get myself back on point and I started taking Destiny out in her stroller everyday. Within six months I had walked all that weight off. After that you couldn't tell me nothing, including Rico. I went from being a sad, miserable bitch to a baller bitch.

Coming Soon

P.O. Box 912
Collierville, TN 38027

A KING PRODUCTION

www.joydejaking.com
@preciouscummingsofficial

ORDER FORM

Name:

Address:

City/State:

Zip:

QUANTITY	TITLES	PRICE	TOTAL
	Bitch	$17.99	
	Bitch Reloaded	$17.99	
	The Bitch Is Back	$17.99	
	Queen Bitch	$17.99	
	Last Bitch Standing	$17.99	
	Superstar	$17.99	
	Ride Wit' Me	$17.99	
	Ride Wit' Me Part 2	$17.99	
	Stackin' Paper	$17.99	
	Trife Life To Lavish	$17.99	
	Trife Life To Lavish II	$17.99	
	Stackin' Paper II	$17.99	
	Rich or Famous	$17.99	
	Rich or Famous Part 2	$17.99	
	Rich or Famous Part 3	$17.99	
	Bitch A New Beginning	$17.99	
	Mafia Princess Part 1	$17.99	
	Mafia Princess Part 2	$17.99	
	Mafia Princess Part 3	$17.99	
	Mafia Princess Part 4	$17.99	
	Mafia Princess Part 5	$17.99	
	Boss Bitch	$17.99	
	Baller Bitches Vol. 1	$17.99	
	Baller Bitches Vol. 2	$17.99	
	Baller Bitches Vol. 3	$17.99	
	Bad Bitch	$17.99	
	Still The Baddest Bitch	$17.99	
	Power	$17.99	
	Power Part 2	$17.99	
	Drake	$17.99	
	Drake Part 2	$17.99	
	Female Hustler	$17.99	
	Female Hustler Part 2	$17.99	

QUANTITY	TITLES	PRICE	TOTAL
	Female Hustler Part 3	$17.99	
	Female Hustler Part 4	$17.99	
	Female Hustler Part 5	$17.99	
	Female Hustler Part 6	$17.99	
	Princess Fever "Birthday Bash"	$6.00	
	Nico Carter The Men Of The Bitch Series	$17.99	
	Bitch The Beginning Of The End	$17.99	
	Supreme...Men Of The Bitch Series	$17.99	
	Bitch The Final Chapter	$17.99	
	Stackin' Paper III	$17.99	
	Men Of The Bitch Series And The Women Who Love Them	$17.99	
	Coke Like The 80s	$17.99	
	Baller Bitches The Reunion Vol. 4	$17.99	
	Stackin' Paper IV	$17.99	
	The Legacy	$17.99	
	Lovin' Thy Enemy	$17.99	
	Stackin' Paper V	$17.99	
	The Legacy Part 2	$17.99	
	Assassins - Episode 1	$12.99	
	Assassins - Episode 2	$12.99	
	Assassins - Episode 3	$12.99	
	Bitch Chronicles	$40.00	
	So Hood So Rich	$17.99	
	Stackin' Paper VI	$17.99	
	Female Hustler Part 7	$17.99	
	Toxic...	$12.99	
	Stackin' Paper VII	$17.99	
	Sugar Babies...	$12.99	
	Deadly Divorce...	$12.99	
	The Legacy Part 3	$17.99	
	BITCH The Story of Precious Cummings	$17.99	
	Mastermind...	$12.99	
	Stackin' Paper VIII	$17.99	
	Stackin' Paper Holiday	$12.99	
	Mastermind 2...	$12.99	
	Baller Bitches Vol. 5	$17.99	
	Mastermind 3...	$12.99	

Shipping/Handling (Via Priority Mail) $9.85 1-3 Books, $18.40 4-10 Books. For 11 or more $24.75.
Total: $_____ **FORMS OF ACCEPTED PAYMENTS:** Certified or government issued checks and money Orders, all mail in orders take 5-7 Business days to be delivered

www.ingramcontent.com/pod-product-compliance
Lightning Source LLC
Chambersburg PA
CBHW022036220526
45357CB00059B/286